MW00577838

BY LILLIAM RIVERA

The Education of Margot Sanchez

Dealing in Dreams

Never Look Back

We Light Up the Sky

Tiny Threads

TINY THREADS

TINY THREADS

A NOVEL

LILLIAM RIVERA

NEW YORK

Tiny Threads is a work of fiction.
Names, places, and incidents either are products of the author's imagination or are used fictitiously. Any resemblance to actual events, locales, or persons, living or dead, is entirely coincidental.

Published in the United States by Del Rey, an imprint of Random House, a division of Penguin Random House LLC, New York.

Del Rey and the Circle colophon are registered trademarks of Penguin Random House LLC.

Hardback ISBN 978-0-593-60047-4
Ebook ISBN 978-0-593-60048-1

Printed in the United States of America on acid-free paper

randomhousebooks.com

2 4 6 8 9 7 5 3 1

First Edition

Book design by Edwin A. Vazquez

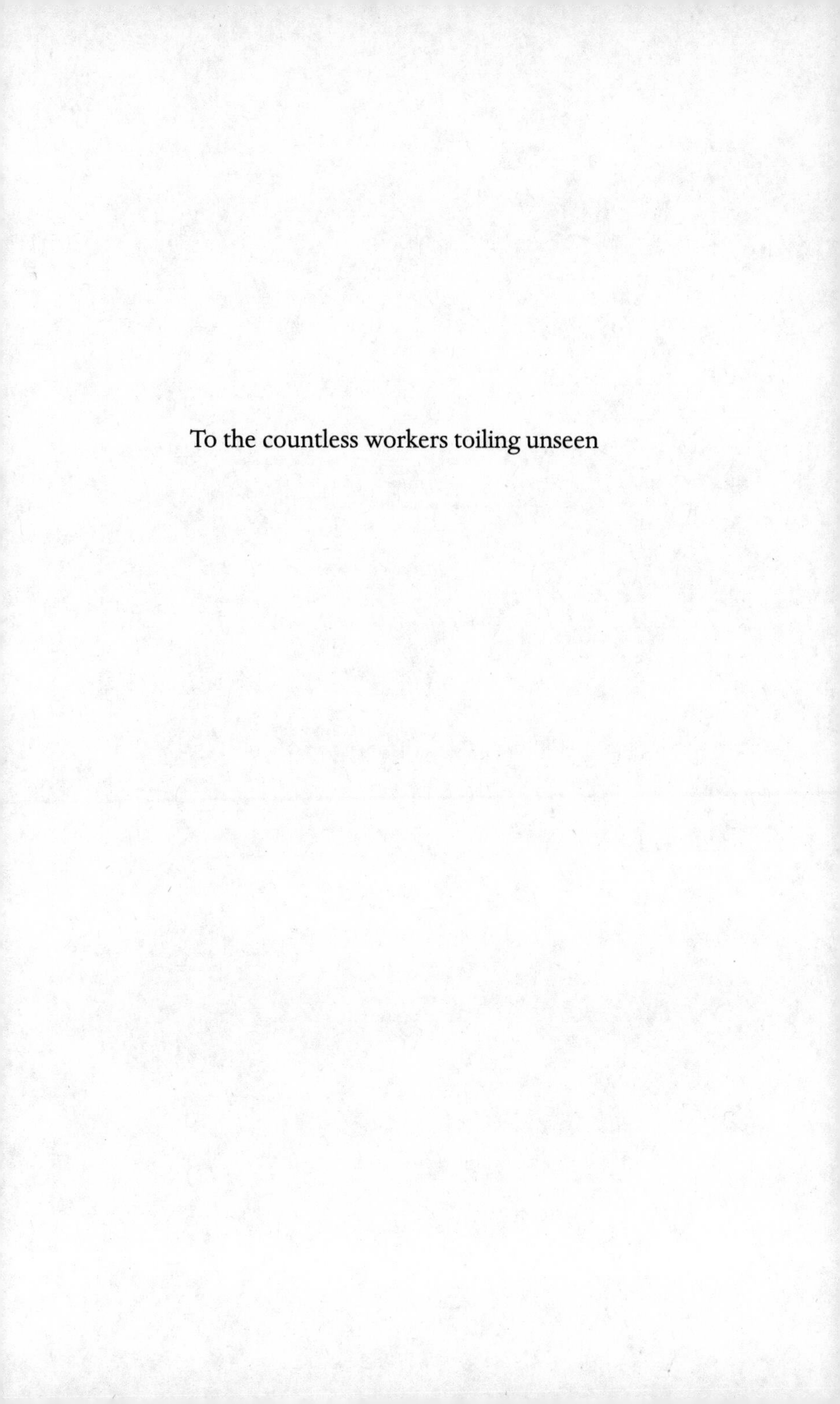

To the countless workers toiling unseen

TINY THREADS

Prologue

The huskiness of his voice reminds her of the men back home, of tobacco and sweat. This is what draws her to him, the earthiness of his scent interlaced with the sweetness of the sprigs of lavender he carries in his pocket like a secret. The flower is for her alone, a gift he gives her whenever he enters the shop. When she lies down to sleep on the hard cot, she inhales deeply the perfume of smoke and lavender that nestles in the waves of her hair. The fragrance replaces the strawberries that once stained her fingers.

The dress she wears that night is too big for her slender frame. She always admired the intricate design of the vibrant red gown and the richness of the silk chiffon fabric complete with a tiny leather flower gracing the back of the neck. Wearing the corset underneath, she feels restrained yet powerful, the rounded neckline framing her bosom. The dress she borrowed from the shop without the patrona knowing of her deed. It's just for one night, and she'll return it to where it belongs.

She holds the white opera gloves in one hand, still unsure if she should wear them or be less formal. The gloves were left behind by one of the customers. She's never been allowed to greet the patrons, has always been tucked away in the back, sewing by hand or cutting the fabric, doing what the patrona asks of her. Not tonight.

Tonight, she'll be seen with him.

"Encantadora," he says when they meet in their agreed-upon corner away from the shop. The patrona warned all the girls to keep away from the important townsfolk, but what does that God-fearing old woman know of these things? She's nothing like the patrona.

"La zorrita, zorrita, señores, se fue a la loma . . ."

He leads her toward the bright lights and the sound of a woman singing. She's never once entered the saloon at this hour. The only time she's seen the inside of the place was late one morning when the saloon owner's wife wanted her dress mended. That day, silent workers swept away the aftermath of a rambunctious night, but the pungent smell of vomit still lingered. She never once looked at the owner's wife while she worked on the dress, but now her chin is raised as everyone greets the man with lively handshakes and hints of fear. The women also nod at her as a greeting and she does the same. They're judging her, but tonight, she's one of them.

She's handed a drink and the man approves when she empties the glass without hesitation. So many people are pressed against each other, drinking and singing loudly alongside a woman strumming the guitar, her cheeks and lips stained red.

"Here." He fills her glass again. Imbibing spirits has always been forbidden to her, but so is everything about this moment—the borrowed, ill-fitting dress, her too-tight shoes that don't match, and the gloves that seem so ridiculously out of place now. So prim and proper. So pure. She gulps down the concoction, allowing it to warm her body, loosening her limbs. Soon the crowd moves outside, toward the back of the saloon.

"This way, sir," a boy says. "We have your seats ready, front and center!"

They flow along with the crowd and she giggles at the sight of the madness, how the townspeople are letting go of their Sunday morning demeanor, the one she witnesses when she attends mass. The churchgoers crowd around the outdoor boxing ring, situating themselves on wooden benches.

"Ladies and gentlemen! In this corner you have the undefeated fighter of all of California!"

The crowd is restless, itching for something vile to happen. The fight commences and all around her everyone shouts while the room begins to spin. She covers her face at every punch and he teases her for it.

He leans in and whispers in her ear. "You don't like it. Too brutal for you. Let me take you somewhere quieter." The man has such gentle eyes.

There's a slight chill in the air and she draws nearer to his warmth. He caresses her fingers as he leads her away from the crowd to a barn.

"You're not like the others in the shop, are you?" he asks and she searches for the right word to say. The language is still so strange. The words sometimes just lay on her tongue like a lump.

"Diferente," she says at first, then corrects herself. "Different."

She holds her breath when he draws nearer.

His caresses take a different tone and at first she welcomes the sudden change. His large hand firmly holds the back of her neck, the same way she would hold a cat. But his touch becomes rougher, hurtful. She doesn't recognize this side of him, but it's too late. When she tries to back away, the slap across her face stings. She drops the gloves on the muddy floor.

"La zorrita, zorrita, señores, se fue a . . ."

Outside the singing continues, intermingled with the screams of the people wanting more blood. All the while, he does such monstrous things to her. Her body no longer exists. It becomes a foreign object, a tool, a meal. Teeth marks on her skin. Chunks of hair floating. Thrusting and laughter. Others soon join, and the night will be endless, filled with such relentless pain.

Later, cloven hooves will climb over her bare legs and atop her chest. There will be so many.

She never screams, not once, only grunts.

When I find it, I'll pull that garment
from its hanger like I'm choosing a body
to carry me into this world, through
the birth-cries and the love-cries too,
and I'll wear it like bones, like skin . . .

—"What Do Women Want,"
Kim Addonizio

CHAPTER 1

December 4

Samara's first day

The lobby is all dark furniture with hard edges and luminous glass walls, except for the piece of art located above the reception desk. Samara recalls reading how the legendary fashion designer Antonio Mota, her new boss, acquired this artwork by the late Cuban artist Ana Mendieta for an exorbitant amount of money. The piece, titled *Color Photo of Earth,* depicts the artist covered in green grass and white flowers. In the article, Antonio said the image spoke to him. "Even in death, Ana's message lives on." The banal-enough statement became the pull quote for the article. Some say Mendieta was pushed out the window by her jealous lover, artist Carl Andre. It's interesting how the striking photo became a print on a pencil skirt Antonio sent down the runway last season. If Ana were still alive, would she have approved?—a question the reporter failed to ask.

"Hi, I'm here to see—"

The receptionist stands.

"Good morning, you must be Samara. Welcome! We're so

happy to have you be a part of our family. My name is Lake Montoya."

Lake is tall and thin with long black hair framing her profile. She wears all black, from the designer's fall collection: a long, clinging silk skirt and a form-fitting blazer with severe, pointy shoulders.

Samara spent the last couple of months committing to memory the various collections and the themes associated with each. Antonio started off in New York in the late seventies with violent, complicated designs that rarely translated into sales. Only a select few bold personalities were able to wear them. He eventually conquered Paris with his less intense creations, but as the years went by, his collections became more and more diluted. They became safe. Easy. After the line for Target came out, his edge was gone. He wants—no, needs—to return to his roots.

The receptionist gestures toward Samara's luggage. A tattoo of an anatomical heart peeks out from her right wrist. "I can take that from you and store it, if you like. How was your flight?"

The place is library-quiet. Only slight murmurings can be heard above the soft, ambient music. There's a whiff of the woodsy and grounding smell of palo santo. The eponymous fragrance is new for the company as they expand into other verticals. Samara's mind can't stop working overtime naming each of the new products. She may have secured the job, but her testing period has begun.

"It was fine," Samara says. "No crying babies, thank God."

Her voice changes to her "white girl voice." When she's with family and friends, her jaw relaxes and her speech drops to a lower octave. It's deeper, guttural. Her white voice is higher, more controlled.

"Antonio should be arriving soon."

"Great. Is there a restroom I can use?"

Samara follows Lake, admiring her towering flatforms. Lake takes a quick left and presses her hand against a silk-screen wallpaper based off of one of Antonio's textile patterns to reveal a hidden door. Samara enters the spacious bathroom with toiletries displayed hotel-style.

Inside, she adjusts her sheer Helmut Lang top and tucks it into her Chanel sailor pants. Her style has always been very Italian mobster princess/hip-hop queen, rocking Nike high-tops and her signature large nameplate hoop earrings. Vintage aviator sunglasses sit atop her straightened brown hair. Samara dresses high and low—mostly low . . . always low—but she's learned to mask the cheap by sprinkling in designer brands here and there. It's how she's been rolling even while living rent-free with her nosy Cuban family in Jersey. Working as a journalist meant being knee-deep in delayed checks courtesy of unreliable freelance gigs.

Moving away from journalism to work behind the scenes with a designer is what excited Samara most about her new position. She has such deep respect for anyone who can manipulate fabric to convey desire or violence. And it all began with a simple sketch and ended with the wearer of the fashion piece becoming a translator of the designer's vision. As Executive Director, Global Brand Voice, Samara can help articulate that visual conversation, try to capture what the designer wants to convey to the masses, and with her input, help shape his message.

Some in the industry thought her too inexperienced for the title. But at twenty-five, Samara was the only fool still living at home instead of with friends crammed into a small apartment in the city no one could afford. So no matter what people said, this was *her* moment to carve her own space.

Moving to California in December meant she could give Jersey winters—and certain recent fucked-up events that almost destroyed her—the middle finger.

"Stop Sleeping on Vernon" was the title of the *New York Times* Style feature Samara wrote six months ago, covering how designer brands were setting up shop in the once industrial city of Vernon, California. Located southeast from downtown, just ten minutes away, Vernon is the new L.A., and now it is her new home.

"Where is she?" A commanding voice resonates across the office.

Samara steps out of the bathroom and places one hand in her pocket. Her headache from the tiny liquor bottles she consumed on her flight is mostly gone. She's as alert as can be with a hangover. She walks back to the reception desk.

"You're finally here," Antonio loudly says, breaking the silence with his deep voice.

Antonio's turning sixty-five this year, although people say he's secretly way older, especially since he's always so coy about revealing his age in interviews. He's lucky to be both beautiful and ageless in that Latino way, with surgeries also keeping his face baby smooth. There's no judgment from Samara about that.

They hug and do a kiss on each cheek. He holds a small stack of notes, phone messages, and a green juice.

"I'm so happy to see you," he says, then addresses the receptionist. "Conference room."

Lake nods. "It's all set up." She presses a button and makes an announcement on the intercom for everyone to meet in fifteen minutes.

Antonio leads Samara to his large expanse of an office. This is not where he sketches. He prefers to work alongside the junior assistant designers he hires in the open floor plan. This office is purely ego, to showcase more art pieces, but it's not the art he's acquired that draws the eye when entering. Instead, it's the art he created: the dress form that showcases his first major design. The Ramona.

Samara walks up to the dress and admires it, finally seeing it in person after reading so much about it. The garment itself combines intricate lacework and leather in vampire red with a plunging neckline revealing an exposed breast. The skirt has a steel-wired hoop, creating a structured bustle with balloon sleeves. Motifs from nature, of flowers and dragonflies, travel up and down the dress. The lacework juxtaposed against the leather became Antonio's signature style. The gown is named after Antonio's great ancestor, the matriarch who forged a new life in California at the turn of the century after leaving Europe.

"Antonio, no one can ever come close to replicating your designs," Samara says while caressing the leather flowers.

"They always try," he answers with a chuckle.

Samara fell in love with how Antonio found ways to fold violence with beauty. At his first show in Paris, Antonio asked two model friends to end the show with one covered in bloodred paint and wearing a thin silk chemise and the other wearing The Ramona. When the model wearing The Ramona pretended to strike at the blood-drenched woman, as Antonio had instructed her to do backstage just minutes before she stepped on the runway, the crowd went wild. He named the show *La Venganza*. Critics loved the boldness of it, how he featured white models subservient to the indigenous-looking ones, for once flipping the script. Although he was raised in New York, ten years ago

Antonio traced his roots to California. It's why he landed in Vernon. His actual percentage may scream Mexican, but he never fails to bring up how connected he is to his Basque side—the Ramona side.

"Are you settled in your new apartment?" Antonio asks, pouring a cup of tea for her. Samara joins him on the couch.

"Not yet. I will after I leave today."

"You didn't have to come here right away. You could have stopped first at your place. I'm not that evil."

Samara grins. This is definitely a trick. Antonio had insisted she take the earliest flight in and come directly to the office from the airport. For this year's Fall/Winter collection, Antonio will be simultaneously streaming two live runway shows on the same day: one in Vernon, immediately followed by the other in New York's Bryant Park. The date is set for February 10, just two months away, and her hiring as Global Brand Voice is evidence of its importance. The newly formed title oversees creative content across all channels. It's on her to make sure the designer's edge is consistently conveyed in every single consumer-facing sentence—be it digital or retail. Samara even pulled some strings to get press on her new position. They posed together for *WWD:* the upstart writer and the legendary designer.

"We have so much to do, don't we? The next two months will go like *that*." She snaps her fingers. "February will be here in no time and everyone will only be talking about you."

Some in the industry think Mota should have focused on the more important September show but Antonio has never been one to do the expected. He insists on placing Vernon on the fashion world's map on his own timeline, no matter what the critics say.

"I can't wait for them to meet you," he says, affectionately squeezing her hand.

THE CONFERENCE ROOM is filled with eager eyes. The workers in the room are mostly white and that disappoints Samara, although it doesn't surprise her. She was hoping Antonio would be more inclusive, especially in California of all places. And maybe she was also wishing there would be another Latina at her level she could connect with, but that won't be happening.

"Let's welcome Samara Martín to The Saprophyte!"

Antonio doesn't pronounce her last name the way she does. Samara becomes Martin, not Mar*teen,* but she doesn't correct him.

The Saprophyte is what Antonio christened the fashion house when he first opened it. Samara likes the specificity of the word after looking up the definition. Everyone in the industry needs a gimmick, including Antonio. Hers is going to be this mask of stability she'll wear, hoping what she left in Jersey will stay there and not rear its ugly head in her adopted city.

This is what she wanted for herself: to be as close to a true artist like Mota as possible so that his spotlight will spill onto her too. She's ready to let go of her grief and be radiant in this new chapter of her life, where no one knows her history, only the story she chooses to tell.

Samara smiles at those in the room and basks in being the center of attention, all eyes on her.

CHAPTER 2

"Here you are." Antonio unlocks the door to Samara's office. The room is small, not grandiose like his, but still, it's Samara's own space, something she barely had in Jersey. The furniture is black and so slick she can see her reflection. On the walls are framed images of Mota's previous runway shows. Two sealed windows overlook the courtyard. She recognizes the enclosure from photo shoots: a lot of green foliage with palm trees and large potted monstera plants.

"It's perfect!" she exclaims.

Samara places her bag down beside a bottle of green juice. She notices how everyone's desk has the same beverage, the breakfast of choice.

After the hour-long meeting, Antonio insists on giving her the tour of the massive fashion house instead of the HR rep. The one-story building is thirty thousand square feet, employs over a hundred workers, and even features a distribution center.

The Saprophyte is divided into two sections, with the financial side, mostly men in business suits, located in the far left of the building. He calls that wing "the money" and whisks her past their offices lined up against the wall.

The creative side is to the right and it's what he's eager to show her.

"Come." Antonio stands underneath the frame of her office door and makes room for her. They both stare out into the open floor plan.

"This is the heart of The Saprophyte, the Design Department," Antonio says as he sweeps his hand across like a king presenting his realm. "You can ask to see anything."

Elevated wooden tables are sprinkled across the expansive workroom. Junior designers drape fabric on erect body forms or perfect sketches on their computers. The tables face Antonio's office, making it easy for him to be connected to what is being done to his designs.

"The red door in the corner there? That's the Library, where all the archives are stored. The archives are going to be important to you. And beyond that is Shipping and Receiving. But before we get there, let me show you what we like to call Seamstress Row."

Roughly twenty seamstresses sit around two very long conference tables, each seated in front of a sewing machine. When negotiating for her job, one of the points Samara insisted on was her being placed near the seamstresses and here they are, only a few steps away from her office. The buzzing from the machines punctuates the lively chatter between the ladies of various ages. To her, it's the sound of love and safety.

Antonio gestures for her to follow.

"Señoras, this is Samara Martín," Antonio announces to the

room. Most of the women before her are brown. Finally, the Latinas she was hoping to see in the conference room are actually all here. "Dolores Lara will be your go-to person."

Dolores wears her gray hair in a severe bun. Around her neck lies a measuring tape. On her wrist are clothing pins at the ready. Dolores's lips are painted pink and although she's smiling, her eyes convey something else to Samara. A look of disapproval, perhaps. Her focus only intensifies when Antonio leaves them to have a discussion with one of his designers.

"Samara Martín." Dolores rolls her name around her tongue. "¿De dónde eres? ¿De España?"

"I'm sorry," Samara says, with a nervous laugh. "My Spanish is not great." This is the one thing her parents fought with Abuela Lola. Being bilingual was important to her grandmother but not to her parents.

Dolores repeats the question in English.

"From New York. Jersey City. My family is from Cuba."

The seamstress takes hold of the measuring tape and lifts it from around her neck. The tape becomes taut around her fingers.

"¿Cubana?" she asks.

"Sí, cubana. My grandmother lived and worked in Vernon before, en las factorías," Samara says, a little too eager. "She was a seamstress at the Celis Knitting Mills. Have you heard of them?"

"Of course. I know the Celis family well." Dolores sounds dismissive, but Samara continues.

"It's funny. Her name is Dolores too like yours. I mean, it was." Connecting with the seamstresses is important to Samara in a way she can't explain, but her laugh is too awkward. Too green. "Abuela Lola. That was what I called her."

The woman's nod is barely there.

Samara tries to shake off this sinking feeling by focusing on the garment the seamstress next to Dolores is working on. She too wears her hair in a tight bun, carefully secured with bobby pins. Samara leans over the older woman to admire the cross-stitch pattern she employs. The seamstress stops the machine and faces her with an expressionless look.

"I'm sorry." Samara sounds weak, even more so because she said it in her white voice. Sweat pools under her armpits and she craves the tiny liquor bottle she kept from her flight in case of any socially awkward emergencies like this one.

Slowly, each of the women seated around the tables stops their machine to stare at her. There's nothing mean about this action—that's not quite the impression she's getting from them—but it's definitely not the welcome she was hoping for either. Their manners are telling her to stick to where she belongs, and it's not here, not with them.

"I should go get settled," Samara says, stepping away. She bumps into the edge of a table and almost loses her footing.

"Be careful," a young seamstress says, offering her a hand. A glint from a silver cross pokes out from her plain white blouse. The woman displays a sympathetic smile—a tiny ray of hope. Samara wants to ask her to have some tea with her in her office, to exchange numbers, or to schedule a lunch already. She's that desperate.

Dolores makes a clucking sound. The kind seamstress drops her eyes back to her machine.

Cheeks flushed, Samara quickly returns to her office. She opens the green juice but stops short of emptying the liquor bottle into it.

She had hoped the seamstresses would be her connection to her grandmother, to the feeling of being protected. Samara hates how needy she is, wanting affection from strangers she just met.

When she told Angie she was leaving, her friend had predicted Samara wouldn't last long out west. "You're too Jersey. There's no way you're going to fit in," Angie said. "You're going to miss all of this."

Samara reaches into her leather tote and pulls out the picture of Abuela Lola. She places the framed photo on her desk. The essay about her grandmother's life was the second story Samara published about Vernon, this time for the L.A. *Times*. It was her most personal work. She wrote how at fifteen, Abuela Lola left Cuba and landed in Vernon, California, instead of Echo Park, where most of the Cuban population converged. Sponsored by her Uncle Francisco, she was meant to help his wife with their three kids, but Abuela Lola made herself indispensable mending work uniforms for the neighbors so they didn't have to buy new ones. Word got out and Abuela Lola was sewing dresses and suits. Francisco couldn't stop her, although he tried. Soon, she joined the others finding work at the factories.

Fashion history marks Celis Knitting Mills as the largest knitting mill on the West Coast. Owned by the Celis family, Knitting Mills was where Abuela Lola truly shined, although she would never get the recognition she and so many workers deserved. The essay was Samara's tribute to the hardworking seamstresses, the unsung alchemists who never take center stage but are constantly breathing life into fabrics.

When she wrote it Samara kept thinking of the many fingers pressing up against the form, the intimacy of body and fabric manipulated by these women. Samara wanted the focus of the feature to be her grandmother's journey from neighborhood seamstress to eventually working for the major movie studios. It was her way of cementing her family's legacy, the version Samara wanted to present to the world. She's certain this piece was why Antonio noticed her. When Abuela Lola died, the job in Vernon appeared right after, exactly when she needed to get the fuck away from her family. Nothing can hurt her here.

Samara tilts her head back to prevent the tears from falling.

"Stop," she tells herself. There's no room for sad-girl emotions.

"Samara, Antonio's looking for you," one of the junior designers calls to her, putting a pause to her sorrow. She pulls out another item she took with her before leaving Jersey. She didn't know if Abuela Lola wanted her to have them but she nabbed them before anyone else in the family questioned her. She places the silver tailoring scissors in front of the framed photo. It's just a little nothing to remind her of the person who cheered her on when her own mother and friends doubted her. They were probably still placing bets, counting down the days when she'll return to Jersey with her tail between her legs, her experiment failed. But she's not going to let that happen. Antonio's fashion show is going to be a success and no one will mess this up for her.

When she steps out of her office, instead of walking past the seamstresses Samara takes the long way around.

CHAPTER 3

"FAMILY LUNCH IS ready in the cafeteria."

Outside of her door, the seamstresses get up all at once and leave their workstations. The overhead announcement is repeated and Samara feels like she's in some Orwellian institution where a godlike voice recites commands everyone must obey.

"What's going on?" she calls out to Tommy, one of the junior designers who is about to join the mass exodus.

"Family lunch. Everyone eats lunch together," he says. "Let's go!"

"Oh. Is it okay if I take a pass? I'm trying to get organized in here." Her first day on the job seems endless with tours and introductions. She hasn't had a moment to set herself up or even to just take a breather.

"Well, I don't know about that, but whenever Antonio is here, he likes everyone to share a meal. It's important for morale, unity, blah blah blah. Besides, this is a special family lunch, catered just for you."

Lake pops her head in.

"I was just about to come get you," she says. "Is Tommy telling you about family lunch?"

"Yup. One big happy family with a side of dysfunction," he says. Tommy is from San Francisco, Filipino, with strong talent. Of all the designers she's met so far, Samara is certain he'll be the one to break out.

"Shut up, Tommy." Lake lightly pushes him. "You're going to scare Samara."

"Well, if this family lunch doesn't do it, just wait till she gets a whiff of the Vernon perfume." He cackles and walks away.

"The what?" Samara asks.

"Never mind him. Tommy likes to exaggerate," Lake says. "We hope you like Mexican food."

Lake leads Samara past the red door of the archives.

"I can't wait to get into the Library," Samara says.

"We'll have keys made out for you. So, how is your first day going? It must be so overwhelming to move across the States and start somewhere new."

"It's been great," Samara says. "Just need to remember everyone's name, not get lost, move into my new apartment, and so on and so on."

"Well, I have friends who work at other fashion brands and they hate it. Nothing compares. This place is really special. Everyone loves each other."

"That's good to hear."

"Oh yeah, Antonio hates big egos. You either love this place or you leave."

Samara is once again reminded she made the right choice.

There's nothing wrong with supporting an artist, being passionate about their work. Everyone circling around Antonio, elevating him.

"I'm so glad he hired a fellow Cubana for the job."

"Wait, are you Cuban?" Samara asks.

"I was the one who showed Antonio the article you wrote about your abuela. When I read it, I couldn't stop crying. And the photo they took . . ." Lake places her hand over her heart.

When the photographer came to take Abuela Lola's portrait, Samara had coated her grandmother's fingers with the fanciest lotion she had. For once Abuela Lola was the model, not just the seamstress, and she loved the attention. Her grandmother felt so important posing in a dress she designed herself.

Samara is so touched by what Lake says that her eyes well up just thinking of how much she misses holding Abuela Lola's hand.

"Thank you. That means a lot."

Lake squeezes Samara's arm. "We have to stick together. If you need anything, I'm always available. Somos familia."

The grief Samara carries recedes further in her body. After the encounter with the seamstresses, this kind gesture is what Samara needed. She has never really worked full time anywhere, just long-term freelance gigs that had her under contract with one client for a few months. Nothing this serious, where she has to commit to entering an office every day. But leaving Jersey was necessary. She needs this, this new family. Samara needs to forget.

A line forms just outside a set of large wooden double doors and Lake deposits Samara at the start of it. The cafeteria is a modern rendition of a cantina with a rustic farmhouse interior design. Sturdy, dark wood tables with matching benches. The food is served buffet-style with lower-level factory workers doubling as servers. As Samara decides on an enchilada with a serving of corn, bypassing the rice and beans, she surveys exactly what a family lunch means to Antonio.

The hierarchy is obvious, with the factory workers seated at tables located at the far end of the cafeteria next to the garbage bins, followed by the office assistants and interns. The seamstresses take up two tables in the center. The rest of the departments follow with Finance, then Human Resources. Lastly, the Design and Marketing Departments crowd around a table where one chair is left empty.

Tommy calls to Samara and motions for her to sit by him. Others at the coveted table include Alex, the creative director, and Sebastian, the in-house photographer, both of them white and just as young as Samara. Antonio soon appears, with Lake carrying a tray behind him. The designer doesn't partake in the buffet. Instead he eats a kale sea salad from Âu Lạc, a vegan restaurant downtown. As soon as he sits, Samara's co-workers lean toward him like magnets. Samara is only a seat away from him, with Tommy, Antonio's favorite designer, sitting between them. She realizes how important her placement is and how she can command his attention.

"Does everyone have lunch together every day?" she asks.

"Yes. It's important we share a meal. I don't like everyone sitting in front of their computers all day," he says. Her co-workers nod their heads, captivated by his every word. "I wanted the cafeteria to have a homely feeling. Everyone next to each other can breed inspiration. You don't get that in other places."

"The design of this room is a nod to the saloons that populated Vernon in the 1900s," Tommy says. "Right, Antonio?"

Behind a bar where drinks can be found are black-and-white framed images of Vernon from that era, proving his point. Women wear bustle-heavy dresses and the men suits and handlebar mustaches. No one smiles in the photos. The city seems covered in layers of dust and hardness but there are also hints of change: Newly constructed storefronts display their wares. A general store. A church. A tailor shop.

"Do any of these buildings exist anymore?" Samara asks.

"Not really, just a couple. The church, Consuelo's Farmhouse," Lake says. "They're bringing in a Whole Foods around the corner from us but it's taking forever."

"We need reminders of our past," Antonio says, barely eating his salad. "It's how we make our creations."

"Especially if the past is violent," Samara adds.

"Isn't it always?" Antonio asks.

The designer shares more insights about the company. Sometimes Samara takes notes on her phone to go over later. Everyone is sweet for the most part, but there's an underlying anxiousness permeating everything. They're all trying so hard to please him. Even Samara gets caught up in it, clocking when Antonio laughs at her jokes or how long she's able to keep his attention.

The lunch is over when the seamstresses stand up and leave the cafeteria in unison.

"How long has Dolores been with you, Antonio?" Samara asks.

"Dolores? She's worked for me for many years. Everyone else here is new, but Dolores has been my rock." Samara finds it comical how Antonio always speaks in sound bites, anticipating that whatever he says will be used later in promo copy. "She's very fashion-forward."

"She is? She seems so . . ." Samara chooses her words carefully. "Well, like you said, like a rock—impenetrable."

Those around her laugh, but it's restrained. Her co-workers don't want to offend Dolores; neither does she.

"They're all religious," Tommy says. "They don't drink or smoke or do anything but watch us in horror as we go wild."

"Wild children they can't control," Antonio says. "There was a time when Dolores wasn't so strict. I have pictures of her as a young woman I'll share with you, Samara. You wouldn't even recognize her."

"I would love to see those."

Lake alerts Antonio about a call. He leaves, and the rest of the group bombards Samara with stories. She laughs along as they recite tales about runway show mishaps and crazy after-parties in secret locations.

"I can't wait for the February show," Samara says.

"Oh forget it. You will not be ready! It's going to be a movie," Tommy says. "Better take extra vitamins because we're going off the rails."

Samara leaves the cafeteria with the rest of the group while the stern men posed stoically in the vintage photos appear to turn their heads to follow her.

CHAPTER 4

Samara teeters on an invisible line: She wants to get really fucked up on the champagne bottle left open on her desk, but she knows she shouldn't. The drinks, along with a box of sweet pastries from a local Cuban bakery, were in celebration of Samara making it through her first day. Samara had attended so many meetings that the people she met eventually blended together. Her mind feels like it's trudging sludge-like through molasses.

She takes another large sip and calculates how many more it would take to properly finish the bottle.

"Almost ready?" Lake asks.

"Just about." Samara grabs the mostly full bottle and carefully places it in the recycling bin, fully aware of how she's wasting good alcohol. "Thank you for offering me a ride."

"Of course," Lake says. "Your place is on my way home."

After Samara locks her office door, they wave goodbye to Tommy, one of the designers staying late.

Seamstress Row is now completely empty, with each sewing machine covered to protect against dust. While Samara entertained in her office, a bell suddenly rang, interrupting her in the middle of a story about Jersey. Across the way, the seamstresses all stood up as one.

"Do they always leave at this hour?" Samara asked Lisa, a copywriter from Brentwood. She and Sean, a graphic designer newly hired from 7 For All Mankind, and Rachel, a product developer and Los Angeles Trade-Technical College graduate from Orange County, comprise Samara's small Marketing team.

"Always. They work nine to five. No more, no less," Lisa said. "Except for when we host private fittings, of course."

"Dolores! Come have some champagne!" Tommy yelled. Dolores turned to them after draping her sweater over her chair.

"No, gracias," she said. "Buenas noches." Samara couldn't stop thinking about how the seamstress didn't acknowledge her during that brief exchange.

She takes hold of the leftover pastries in one hand and her suitcase handle in the other, and follows Lake through hallways, trying to remember signs around the office for when she returns the next day.

"You're going to love The Murphy. A lot of people are trying to get in that building," Lake says. "You're lucky Antonio pulled some strings. It's *the* spot."

Lake rags on downtown L.A. and how dead the scene has become. Vernon is where everyone wants to be, she says. The longer Lake talks, the more Samara feels justified in her decision to move. No matter what her family thinks, there's no denying Samara has landed at the start of the city's ascension.

Before Lake pushes open the exit leading to the parking lot, she turns to Samara with a grave face.

"Prepare yourself," she says in an ominous tone.

Then she pushes the door open.

"Oh my god!" Samara gasps. "What is that?"

The stench is so strong Samara starts to cough. The thickness of the stink turns her stomach. She can't help but gag.

"*That* is the Vernon perfume," Lake says.

The odor is shocking, unimaginable. They walk quickly to Lake's electric Volkswagen, open the trunk, and place Samara's luggage in. Samara covers her nose and mouth and jumps in the passenger seat.

"Why does it smell like something died out there?" she asks.

"It's the slaughterhouse, the one next door to us," Lake says. "A lot of new residents aren't happy with the air quality. This place is probably slowly poisoning us. There's been talk of moving the slaughterhouse, but for now all we can do is try not to breathe in too deeply at certain times of the day."

"You've got to be kidding me."

"Let me show you what we're dealing with," Lake says, laughing. "You won't believe it."

They pull out of the parking lot and make a quick turn.

"Welcome to Vernon," she says as she slows the car down.

Just around the corner from The Saprophyte is Consuelo's Farmhouse, a national brand Samara's seen stocked in supermarkets and featured in corny commercials meant to convince consumers how healthy their meats are. Their ads feature studly farmers and hippie girls working the farm. "A return to the way things used to be" is how they've positioned their brand, or something just as ridiculous.

The block-long factory is covered in vibrant murals depicting an idyllic farm life with a smiling farmer chasing after pigs. As Samara looks closer, the artwork becomes clearer and more nightmarish. Dogs and chickens frolic around the farm with dead eyes. Massive pigs eat their slop with demented grins. The murals must have been created by demonic children.

"This can't be real," Samara says with a nervous chuckle.

"Oh it's real. Consuelo's been here for decades. A Vernon landmark," Lake says. "The person who painted these murals died of a heart attack right after he finished—the very next day. Probably after he realized how ugly they were."

"Or maybe the fumes did him in," Samara jokes. How did she miss this when reporting about Vernon? Had she really been so blinded by the promise of the rising fashion enclave that she'd ignored its decaying aroma?

Lake drives slowly around the block so Samara can get the complete view. "Don't ever bring this up to Antonio. He hates this building so much. He goes into a full rage every time someone reminds him of the eyesore."

As they travel past the main entrance of the building, groups of mostly Latino workers exit, ranging from very young to old.

"Can you imagine being stuck working there?" Lake asks with disgust.

"No," Samara says, but she can. The faces she sees are not family—but they are in some way. The Martíns were once no strangers to factory work. Abuela Lola never mentioned Consuelo's, but she always talked about long hours working in the Knitting Mills for measly pay, even when her work was being shipped to the movie studios. The glamour of Hollywood built by those laboring behind the scenes like Abuela Lola.

Although the windows are closed and Lake has the A/C full blast, Samara can still smell it. She wonders if her clothes are contaminated by the stench. Lake jokes about the slaughterhouse while second thoughts about relocating to Vernon creep into Samara's mind.

CHAPTER 5

THE DOORMAN TO The Murphy greets Samara by immediately taking her luggage.

"Welcome. My name is Raul. I hope you had a relaxing flight." Raul has bushy eyebrows, a squat build, and the face of someone who has been in a few fights. Samara likes him immediately.

When she first read up on The Murphy, Samara loved the history. The Murphy was once a famous saloon in the 1900s known for its bar: over one hundred feet long and once staffed by forty bartenders. Drinking and debauchery were constants. The saloon even had a boxing ring attached to it. And because of this history, there are several photos of boxers in shorts with bare, broad chests in the building's lobby. She wonders if Raul's flattened nose got him the job as the doorman; his rugged Javier Bardem features make him the perfect representative for the building.

"Fifth floor, correct?" Raul asks, pressing the elevator call button. "Just dial zero if you need any assistance."

The elevator is a reproduction of a 1900s lift with ornate iron metalwork, a small upholstered bench, and a mirror. Samara runs her fingers along the ironwork before catching her reflection. The lighting in the elevator is dim and amplifies her haggardness. Samara is tempted to sit down on the tufted velvet bench, but she doesn't think she would be able to get back up. Her body is crashing from being "on" all day.

It takes her a couple of seconds to locate her apartment and another minute to find the right key. The studio is bigger than any of her friends' apartments back in New York at half the rent. Her furniture should be arriving by the end of the week. In the meantime, she's happy to see the mattress she ordered already on the floor with an unopened set of bed sheets atop it.

Samara opens her suitcase and quickly hangs her clothes in the closet. She lines up her bathroom essentials—finally, she doesn't have to share her shampoo and beauty products with her mother, who only used to cluck disapprovingly at her expensive choices. She sets her diffuser near her mattress and places drops of lavender oil into it.

The plan was never to be the last of her friends to still live at home, but that's what happened. When she graduated from Columbia four years ago, she'd planned to join Angie and Carolina in their tiny Manhattan apartment. Although she was lucky that her freelance gigs allowed her the freedom to travel at a moment's notice, the assignments were never consistent enough to cover her share of a lease. And her parents had refused to spot her the first and last months' rent she'd needed to move in the first place. They had this insane idea that Samara could only leave their home when she got a permanent job or got married, whichever came first.

"You'll be back in six months," Caro said to her on Samara's last night in New York, between sips from a flute of pink

Chandon. "You don't belong in the land of blond hair and fake titties."

"Picture this bitch meeting Karen for yoga, or spin, or whatever they're doing out there," Angie chimed in.

"That's not going to happen," Samara insisted. "Give me some credit for being my own person."

"That shit happened to J.Lo," Caro warned. "You ain't that strong."

Angie and Caro high-fived each other and laughed so hard their cackles could be heard above Karol G's "Ay, DiOs Mío!" being played like a sexual proclamation. Samara had always been the one in her circle who never did anything salacious. The tame one who worked out her Catholic school guilt through writing, while her friends lived their ho lives in real time. Instead, Samara just drank too much.

"Well, here's hoping Samara finally, *finally* lands some dick," Angie said, raising her Long Island iced tea for a toast. Caro raised her glass too, adding, "Here's to West Coast dick!" Samara called them bitches as she clinked her glass to theirs. The drinks kept flowing while the toasts got raunchier.

Samara plops onto the mattress and stares at the ceiling of her apartment. There are small imperfections in the paint job, even a crack in a corner, but she can barely hear the neighbors. No one screaming at her. No one cornering her in a crowded hallway. She can't believe she made it. She really had boarded the plane and left the bad behind, where it can never hurt her.

She read in some women's lifestyle magazine that when living in a new home, a ritual is needed to bring forth the right type of energy. You couldn't just show up to a place and expect good things to happen. There was a contract that needed to be made, a seed planted. Right now her apartment is a shell, without furniture and the touches that would scream Samara Martín.

"Let my home be filled with glorious orgasms," she says, sliding her hand down her pants. "Let this be the beginning of my ho chapter."

She recites the mantra until she makes herself come. Then she counts down the days to the fashion show.

"Sixty-eight." Only sixty-eight days to prove herself to Antonio and prove to everyone back in Jersey that leaving was the best decision she's ever made.

Before sleeping, she takes a small sip from the airport bottle, a little celebratory drink to end the night like a boss.

SOMETHING WAKES HER. Samara sits up, disoriented, unaware of where she is or of the time. She stares at the unfamiliar ceiling. This happened to her once before, after spending days staying in various hotels for a story that took her on the road with a musician. The pop singer spoke about the strangeness of sleep, how life on the road meant learning to trick her body into finding home wherever she landed. This meant keeping an orange right beside the bed so that the citrusy smell would remind the singer of her home back in Florida. When she travels, Samara tries to find things that would root her back to her sense of self. The diffuser continues to blow beside her, blanketing the air with lavender, but it's slow in helping her find her center.

"Fuck," she says as she reaches for her phone to check the time. Two in the morning.

Samara walks to the large windows overlooking Main Street. The streets are completely desolate, not a person walking or a car driving by. From where she stands, she can see the Vernon water tower. The tank is graffitied with the letters "RIP" dripping like blood. She lifts open the window and leans her body out, rolling her shoulders. It's so quiet, and she relishes how unlike New York this is. There are no sounds, like a radio playing or people speaking. Silence, for once.

Then she hears something faint. Very faint. A strange sniffling sound like the heavy breathing of an animal. But there's nothing out there. No dog or cat she can see. The noise continues with a rustling accompanying it. Then a grunt. When Samara leans out more, squinting into the barely lit street, the deathly scent rolls in from the slaughterhouse.

Samara slams the window shut, afraid the foul scent will enter her apartment, but the noise stays in her room. Weird gulping sounds. It bothers her so much that she searches for the tiny liquor bottle, only to realize there isn't much left. Not enough to make a dent in her anxiety anyway.

She plays classical music off her phone as loud as she can to drown out the outdoor clamor. She takes an Ambien, finishes the liquor, and lies back down on her mattress. Still, sleep evades her.

CHAPTER 6

December 5

67 DAYS UNTIL THE FASHION SHOW

THE NEXT DAY she decides to wear a full denim outfit: a black tunic with matching pantaboots and a sleeveless, oversized vest dripping with crystal embellishments on the shoulders. Her hair is slicked back, no jewelry or makeup, except for a bloodred lip. She looks like a space alien. The bags under her eyes add to the extraterrestrial ensemble.

Last night's strange noises kept her up. She blames the time zone change and her sleeping pill not working. The crack in the ceiling was her only companion as she waited for the sun to rise and force her to get dressed, get out, and do what she's meant to do in Vernon.

"Good morning," Samara says to the seamstresses already settled in front of their sewing machines. Determined to get on their good side, she opens a box of conchas. "I have a little morning snack for us."

The youngest of the bunch seems happy for the sugar. She's tall with fine black hair. Heavy makeup and overly stenciled eyebrows obscure her fair skin. She's giving Rosalía by way of the East Side. The seamstress moves to take a concha but stops when she notices how the others are waiting for Dolores. Dolores doesn't stop moving a piece of fabric through the machine until Samara stands in front of her.

"I thought you might like this one," she says, holding a concha covered in pink frosting, the only one like it in the box.

Dolores takes the pastry and a napkin and places it on her workstation. She says thank you, but it's barely audible.

"When I was little, I used to hide underneath my grandmother's sewing machine so they couldn't find me," Samara says, leaning against the table. She doesn't know why she's sharing this memory, but the thought of it reminds her of her grandmother's kindness.

Underneath the sewing machine, Samara made sure to surround herself with the things she loved—a doll, broken crayons. Above her, Abuela Lola would work on the designs she took on as commission from the neighbors—quinceañera gowns or cocktail dresses for a special occasion. The sounds the machine made would sometimes lull Samara to sleep. In her dreams, she would overhear conversations not meant for her ears, adult topics too confusing for her to understand.

Clients would visit and say hello to her underneath the desk, calling Samara Abuela's mini-assistant. Before the customers would leave, Abuela Lola would always end the transaction with "Estamos aquí a la orden." She was always of service to the clients, no matter if they were family or strangers.

And there were times when Abuela Lola had words only meant for Samara. Warnings.

"Never listen to men on the first try. They'll hide their intentions from you."

"Always pay attention to signs. Most people ignore the signs, and that's when they get lost."

"Men are most afraid of strong, smart women."

Samara would take notes on what Abuela Lola said like a secretary. She knew the advice was important because it was told only to her and not to her cousins. Abuela Lola was giving her insight that would help her future. These were important keys to success, so her notes, though mostly misspelled scribbles, were codes Samara would need.

"Are you listening to me?" Abuela Lola asked, and Samara would tap on her grandmother's naked toes to reassure her that she heard every word.

"What was your grandmother's name?" the friendlier seamstress asks.

"Abuela Lola. That's what everyone called her. The family, our neighbors, everyone," Samara says. "She had a Singer sewing machine. One of those antique ones that comes attached to the table. They don't make them anymore. She refused to upgrade even when we wanted to buy her a new one. She said they didn't work as well as her brazo derecho. That's what she called her sewing machine, *su brazo derecho.* So funny. She had such a big personality."

The young seamstress has a warm, welcoming energy, unlike Dolores, who doesn't seem excited about the concha or Samara's story.

"Anyway, enjoy!"

Samara walks to the cafeteria for a cup of coffee to go along with her breakfast. The seamstress joins her.

"What's your name again?" Samara asks. "I'm sorry. It's going to take me a minute to remember everyone's name. So many faces."

"My name is Rosa. I'm new here too."

"Oh, like me! I'm not the only one. We can be confused together," she says, and Rosa laughs. "Where did you work before this?"

Rosa crinkles her angular nose. "This is my first job."

"Oh wow."

Shy, Rosa shares little about herself, but Samara doesn't let her off easily. She's from Vernon and graduated from high school a couple of years ago. Her family all work in the factories.

"I want to be a model, but for now I can help with the clothes," Rosa says. "And maybe learn how to be a designer too."

Samara can't help herself. She gives Rosa the once-over. She's tall enough to be a model, and beautiful, but there's nothing unique, nothing that would capture a photographer's eye. But at least she's thin enough to wear Antonio's designs.

"Have you ever thought of going to fashion school?" Samara asks.

"Oh no, I can't afford that."

"Well, you have such great access here. I'm sure you can move into another department." She's not sure at all if this is true. For all she knows, Antonio might like to keep things the way they are. The fact that they hired Samara from the outside instead of hiring within the company says a lot. Sometimes a boss only sees what he wants to see and not the potential of those people on the team. "You can probably ask our photographer if you can assist him, or Tommy, if you want to learn more about designing."

"Dolores wouldn't like that," she says, almost at a whisper. "I shouldn't be bothering you."

"You're not bothering me. You can talk to me whenever you want. We're both new here. We need each other."

When they walk back, Samara catches Dolores eating the pastry.

"It's good, right, Dolores?" she asks.

The woman wipes her mouth with a napkin and goes back to work. Samara lets out a little laugh. The vieja refuses to engage, but that bite from the concha is Samara winning.

"Can someone do me a big favor and open the Library for me?" Samara asks, looking directly at her. "I should be getting a key soon."

"I can do it since you're busy, Dolores!" Rosa eagerly stands, but Dolores dismisses her. Rosa doesn't hide her disappointment.

Samara follows Dolores to the red door. The seamstress unlocks it, flips the light switch on, and steps aside to let her in.

The Library is a surprisingly large walk-in closet that contains every important creation Antonio has made throughout his thirty-plus years as a designer. The walls are adorned with racks of clothing organized by collection. Full-length mirrors on opposite sides lean against the walls while a bookcase enclosed behind glass contains research materials: photography books, art history books, old issues of *Vogue* and *Harper's Bazaar* magazines bound in leather. In the center of the room are cabinets with fabric swatches, buttons, hooks—tiny trinkets organized for easy access, with an iPad cataloging where everything lives.

Before Dolores leaves, Samara stops her.

"I bet you have so many interesting stories behind each of the collections," she says. "Antonio told me you've worked with him for many years."

"No," Dolores says, pressing her lips tight. "The stories are for Antonio to tell."

"But I'm sure you can tell me something. It'll be great to

hear them as part of my research, especially since the show is in less than two months."

Dolores takes another step to the door.

"There's nothing to tell. The clothes speak for themselves," she says. "If you're looking for stories, it's all in here."

"No, what I meant—"

"Make sure to turn off the light and lock the door," Dolores says before leaving.

"Thank you for the concha, Samara. Of course I will share all the stories with you, just pull up a chair," Samara says to herself. "You're like a daughter to me. We're going to be family."

She lets out a long sigh and picks up the iPad.

"I guess it's just you and me," Samara says to the racks of clothes. A cold draft kisses her neck. Her arms become covered in goose bumps.

She spends the rest of the day studying the archives and playing dress-up with Antonio's history. Each design brings her closer to what made him so great. The more brutal the construction, the sexier the wearer became. Iterations of The Ramona are like fingerprints marking his genius. Hours go by as she gently handles each garment. Samara gets used to the cold, even when the tips of her fingers go numb.

CHAPTER 7

SHE FEELS LIKE a walking tape recorder. Samara's responsibility today is to tag along with Antonio and document his day-to-day for a magazine feature. Anyone else would have the PR Department make up a daily routine or give the task of shadowing him to an intern, but not Antonio. Work duties are fluid at The Saprophyte, a principle hidden under the guise of "everyone is a team player, which means everyone gets dirty." Antonio insists on having Samara follow him around to get details of his life in real time, while also seeing how things work at the brand. What she didn't expect was to be a witness to his temper so soon.

"I hate what you're doing here. This is terrible!" Antonio crumples the sketch handed to him by Tommy and tosses it aside. "I don't understand why everyone is so dense. I made myself clear weeks ago."

Only two days into her new job and already he flashes his ugly side. Samara thought she would have at least a couple of weeks before the real Antonio presented himself. He continues to berate Tommy, who just stands there without saying a word.

"Why can't you just do what I asked you to do?" Antonio raises his voice. His fists are closed tight.

"I have a book on my desk you should look at, Tommy. *Everyday Life in California,* in watercolors," Samara says. "I think you might like it."

"Yes, go get that book," Antonio says with disgust. "Do *something.*"

Before Tommy leaves, he picks up the sketch from the floor and sneaks a look of resignation to Samara, a look of "welcome to our world." She offers him a sympathetic nod.

"I do Pilates in the morning and meditate for twenty minutes each day," Antonio says, ignoring how he just yelled at his employee. "I want to start my day refreshed and clear. Body and soul."

Samara writes down what he says, also choosing to overlook what she just witnessed. She confesses how much she needs to start a meditation practice.

"Who's your trainer?" she asks.

"I don't want to give him any press. He's also training Devlyn with a *Y.*"

Samara grimaces. Devlyn is a new designer who creates absurdist clothing in over-the-top theatrical silhouettes. A recent collection included hundreds of porcelain doll heads used as embellishment on a full skirt. Devlyn hosts his own reality show on one of the streams, where he selects the next big designer. Antonio hates him because of what Devlyn said in an interview a couple of years ago, hinting at how Antonio didn't know what women wanted to wear. He's tried to make amends for the oversight, even sending a personalized invite to the show's premiere, but to Antonio, Devlyn is forever blacklisted.

"I heard his show is being canceled," Samara says. This isn't at all true. In fact, the ratings are doing great. She just needs to quickly change the subject to avoid Antonio's bad mood re-emerging.

"No one is watching that trash," Antonio says, and he continues listing his morning rituals.

His current mood board is pinned on the wall behind him so he can easily manipulate the swatches and the tear sheets. There are photos of paintings by Goya, scenes from a war, computer-generated flowers, and a photo close-up of men with diamond-encrusted tears spilling from their eyes.

"MOCA has a great exhibit right now on Goya's Black Paintings," Samara says. "We should go. I haven't been since last year when I flew in to cover their gala. Remember when Seven went pantless?"

The musician Seven and Antonio are roughly the same age, but you wouldn't know it by the way Seven changes her face every season. She debuted her latest look at last year's gala and walked the red carpet wearing nothing but a thong. Her legs looked amazing, but the reporters only talked about her puffy face. In the seventies, the iconic musician was Antonio's muse. He even designed her wedding dress. But like many other artists, she had lost interest in his clothes and moved on to newer, younger designers.

"Send one of the interns and have them take pictures for us."

Antonio always wears black, which is an obvious choice. He has a personal tailor who comes to his house once a week and travels with him to make sure his outfits fit precisely. The only color he allows himself is the chunky gold ring with a bloodred ruby stone he wears on his right index finger, the very same finger he is now pointing at her.

"You need to delegate. You're no longer freelance," he says. "Use the staff to get what you want. You don't want them to be confused as to your standing. You're management now."

Samara is certain he's talking about her bringing in conchas for the seamstresses. She understands the message: He wants her to be firmer and not show weakness.

"Sure, I'll make sure to have them go by the end of the week and then send us all a rundown of the exhibit and how it may or may not translate to your current collection. Break it down to inspiration, current trends, and what the competitors are doing."

She notices a small illustration framed in gold and propped up on a shelf just next to the side of the mood board. The simple pencil sketch is of a young Antonio wearing a hat and standing in front of Caffe Reggio in New York. Only place color is used: red for his lips.

"I love that," Samara says, motioning to the piece.

"If this whole place burns down, that will be the first thing I take." He walks over to the shelf and plucks the frame off of it. With a lint cloth, Antonio wipes dust from the glass and places it back. Samara is surprised he didn't say he would take The Ramona or any of his other more important designs.

"Who drew it?" She figures this could be a new story the press might find compelling enough, since almost everything else has already been reported about Antonio. After all, there's nothing suggestive or interesting about the designer anymore, nothing that would make a person buy his clothes except maybe a taste for nostalgia. It's on Samara to change that.

"Angel. He was a fashion illustrator and we were going to take over the world." The way he regards the sketch with such love, Samara's definitely hit on something intimate, personal. "I was never good with sketching, but Angel was so talented. He was an *artist*. I just had to say a couple of things to him and he knew exactly what to do. We were meant to leave Vernon together. He sketched this when we were dreaming of what our future would be."

"But I thought you grew up in New York and only found out about your Vernon roots recently?" Samara says, confused.

"You're not that gullible, are you? Being from Vernon wasn't glamorous enough, so I made that whole 'raised in New York' life up."

Samara feels foolish for not knowing this. A simple search would have yielded his real history, but he's right: Hustling in New York when you're starting out is sexier.

Antonio continues to share how he and Angel met in high school and eventually lived in a small Vernon apartment. They were both starting out and in love.

"And what happened?"

"He got sick and died, and I lost my mind. I left Vernon because it was broken for me, but every city felt that way. New York, Paris," he says. "I thought I would never be able to come back here, that I would see him on every corner. And maybe I do, but I welcome it now. He's reminding me to return to the person I was. Unafraid."

Samara can't help but think of her own grief.

"You can write that down."

"Oh yeah, right. Sorry." She forgot this isn't about her. This is the story he's selling, and she can relate, because didn't she sell

Abuela Lola's history to a magazine? Didn't that essay get her this very job?

"Vernon is so important to me. It's a really special place, but there's a lot of history I've tried to forget. My family wasn't always there for me, not when they found out who I really was. But that's been told so many times. I'm so bored with it. The story of the boy kicked out of his house, not accepted, urgh. Do you understand?"

"Why come back?" Samara asks. "If this place once caused you pain?"

He stares at her with such seriousness that she feels a little unsettled by it. Maybe she's being too presumptuous by asking, but she's really curious. His answer might help with her own heartache.

"Vernon is also a source of possibility for me. I get to conquer this city the way I did New York and Paris," he says. "This is my home, and I get to burn it down and rebuild it."

Samara's almost on the edge of sharing with Antonio her own history of running away from family. She hasn't spoken to anyone about what happened to her, hasn't allowed herself to even voice it for fear the weight of it will crush her. Instead, she writes down his words.

When Samara finishes the write-up and sends it to him for approval, he deletes all references to Angel and how his family abandoned him. As much as he had wanted to confess to her, in the article itself he's determined to only focus on his Basque roots instead of his Californian ones, on how his Spanish family took hold of this land generations ago and made it their own. The story of his former lover was meant only for Samara and no one else.

"We're introducing the history of my family to the world.

Their struggles," Antonio explains. "I want you to read about my people and go through the archives. They created a life for themselves, leaving behind everything they loved and owned. It's a great immigrant story."

The truth is a European family came to California and literally raided the land and cut out the people who originally lived there, but Samara doesn't share this historical reality with Antonio. Her job is to introduce his new collection, centering on a reimagining of The Ramona dress as a warrior's armor—an embodiment of his family arriving in Vernon and spilling blood. Forget about his one true love, concentrate only on conquest.

A photographer arrives to take Antonio's picture and Samara suggests they go out to the garden. She stays to watch and assures Antonio that he looks good. This season's fashion show is more than just a return. It's a reminder to everyone of his legacy. It's on Samara to shake the cobwebs from his history and make it gleam like new.

"The answers are in the archives," he repeats.

"Don't worry, Antonio, I plan to live there," she says. "Everyone's going to be reminded just who the fuck you are."

He displays the tiniest smirk before posing. The vibrant reds and pinks from the hanging bougainvillea frame his face beautifully like a painting. While the photographer clicks away, a small yellow worm on a leaf wiggles toward Antonio and lands on his suit.

"There's a little something—" Samara says and cups it between her hands before Antonio notices.

"Thank you, Samara," he says. "I knew you would have a good eye."

When she opens the palm of her hand, she discovers that it's not a worm at all, but a maggot. The ugly thing appears to want to go back to Antonio. She drops the maggot to the ground and steps on it, disgusted by the stain it leaves behind. Samara eyes her surroundings with suspicion, afraid maggots will land on her too.

CHAPTER 8

SAMARA FINDS THE DIFFERENCES between Vernon and Jersey interesting, but not in the "East Coast is the best coast" obnoxious way people get when they live elsewhere. There are little things she misses, like having access to her favorite bodega, or a solid sense of direction. She's always a little off when it comes to figuring out which way to go. The street signs are not as intuitive here, but she's allowing herself grace and time to figure it out. Each day she takes a different route to explore her new neighborhood. So when Tommy offers to give her a ride home after they both find themselves working late, she opts to walk instead.

"Tell me you're from New York without telling me," he says before getting into his car.

"It's not that far to get to The Murphy," she explains. "And it's so nice outside."

"Sure. Get those steps in," he teases. "I'll see you tomorrow."

Although it's only nine o'clock, the streets are empty, and

because of this, Samara brings Abuela Lola's scissors along for protection. She may be excited about the casualness of her new home, but she's not stupid. At least in New York, this hour would be filled with people heading to the train or getting a bite to eat. Samara rarely encounters anyone during her walks except for maybe the workers from Consuelo's Farmhouse waiting for a ride to arrive. She once saw an opossum and screamed, then laughed because the animal was way more scared of her than the other way around.

The silence is a welcome change from the commotion she always lived in. There was a time when Samara hid in a closet to conduct an interview—the only quiet space in her family's home for her to work her freelance life. Not that everything is perfect in Vernon. During her explorations she'll find herself on the street after a sidewalk abruptly ends. City planners apparently giving up. Vernon still needs to break free from its industrial past, where its streets were built to cater to massive trucks. It's not pedestrian-friendly at all. The city needs more trees, more touches of livability. More *people*.

Her Prada loafers don't make much noise and she likes the way her A-line Mota skirt switches against her legs in a sensual manner. Dressing up for work is something she enjoys. If she's not getting approval from Antonio or from her co-workers, then she's failed at amping up her fashion. Her appearances are daily assessments she has to pass. Compliments are the gold stars she collects.

Only a couple of long avenues left to make it to The Murphy. She thinks about the money she's saving by walking and what a good environmental citizen she is while also glancing at her phone to heart items on Net-a-Porter that she has her eye on purchasing. There are still so many things she needs for the apartment. As of late she's been paying attention to emerging artists, asking Antonio who he loves and why. She wants to purchase her first art piece soon and then invite people over so they can stare at it, adding "gallery girl" to her growing resume.

As she rounds a corner, her eyes catch a glint of light twinkling. She can't quite make the object out at first, but soon it comes into focus.

A long silver meat hook hangs off a telephone wire. Dangling from the hook is an empty wooden fruit crate. The box sways back and forth creating an eerie sound, almost like an out-of-tune guitar string. The hook is so severe, strangely new, not rusty in any way. In contrast, the wooden crate is old and stained. The label on the crate is barely legible, with a faded illustration of a woman with short, tight curls wearing a type of caricatured Mexican folklore costume with bells dangling from the sleeves. Her cleavage heaves forward, but it's her face that has Samara transfixed. A garish green color covers her cheeks, causing the face to appear ghoulish. Dead.

The crate keeps swaying. Then a whimpering sound emerges from a nearby bush. The bush trembles and the noise becomes louder. The hook moves faster. The movement more severe. The crate now rocks back and forth.

"What the hell?" Samara asks, wondering if another opossum is hidden in the bush, waiting to jump out. Like a fool, she doesn't move, even when the rocking becomes more violent.

The pungent stink from the slaughterhouse reaches her nostrils and her knees go weak. Samara tries to shield herself from the stench by covering her mouth and nose. The Vernon perfume hasn't been bothering her too greatly. She's usually able to avoid it. There's something of a timetable to when it drenches the air and she tries to follow that schedule. But this is the first time Samara is being polluted with it on her walk home. The scent is so thick and moist, like nothing she's ever encountered before—and she's taken the subway during New York heat waves. There's no wind and yet the smell is so powerful.

The whimpering grows louder, more precise. Something is coming. Samara digs in her purse and takes out Abuela's scissors. The tremor in her hand causes the metal to catch the light of the moon, and it gleams just like the swinging hook. Samara doesn't understand how the crate continues to sway or what's jostling the bush.

"Who's there?" she asks, not in her white voice but in her Jersey accent. Her breath quickens and her heart rises in her chest. "Hello?"

Suddenly, the wooden crate drops in front of her. Samara screams and runs like someone is chasing her, clutching the scissors in her tight fist. When The Murphy comes into view, she rushes toward the entrance.

"You look like you saw a ghost," Raul says, holding the door for her. He drops his grin when Samara glares back. "Are you okay?"

"No, I'm not," she says. Samara tries to shake it off, steadies her ragged breathing. Eventually she chuckles, picturing what she must have looked like running like a madwoman down an empty street.

"It's probably not a good thing for you to walk by yourself at night," he says.

"I walk everywhere in New York." She wipes the sweat off her forehead. Her hands still shake.

"Vernon isn't like New York," Raul says.

"The only thing different about Vernon is the disgusting smell from the slaughterhouse."

"You get used to it," Raul says, pressing the elevator call button for her. "I don't even smell it anymore."

"I don't think I'll ever get used to it," she says.

Samara says good night to Raul and thinks about the dangling hook as the elevator deposits her onto her floor.

CHAPTER 9

Samara says hello to Joseph the doorman, who only nods back a response. Like Raul, this doorman has a boxer's build with a smashed-up nose and a facial scar on his chin to perfect his pugilist style. But unlike Raul, this doorman isn't friendly. Raul always seems to give her a tiny bit of Vernon history or a tip for where to find the best food. And maybe because she usually sees Raul in the evenings or at night, their chats feel just a bit more intimate. Raul seems to be checking in on her, but Joseph couldn't care less. He's way more attentive to the other residents, especially right now to the white woman exiting the lobby with her tiny Yorkshire terrier. Joseph's eager to hold the door open for her and her dog.

By contrast, the doorman rarely looks at her. Samara's invisible, not worthy enough to be acknowledged, but this doesn't stop her from getting in his face anyway when she needs something.

"Do you know of any gift shops nearby, a florist maybe?" she asks.

The white man furrows his bushy eyebrows. "Vernon Florists is a five-minute drive from here," he says, then closes the door behind him before she can ask him in which direction.

"Useless," she says, taking out her phone and bringing up the GPS.

Before leaving work yesterday, Antonio called her in to his office to ask what her plans were for the weekend, which led to dinner tonight at his place. She didn't share this news with her co-workers. Samara wants to have a story to tell on Monday, of how differently she spent her days off than they did.

The California sun is obscured by clouds, the cool December weather perfect. Samara walks up Main Street toward work. "Coming Soon" signs pepper empty storefronts. Another restaurant. New coffee shops.

She moved at the right moment. Soon Vernon will be like Brooklyn with a Starbucks and a Target on every corner.

Trucks still inhabit the road but not as intensely as they do during the week. She clocks an open liquor store with lottery tickets ready for purchase and a taco truck about to drive away from it.

So much of her time at work is spent figuring out who she can or cannot befriend. So many meetings blur into one long-ass meeting filled with talking heads and emails. Not that she's complaining. She loves the excitement of it, the newness, but it's also nice to linger.

"Oh damn," Samara says when she reaches Vernon Florists only to discover it's closed. Why didn't that asshole doorman warn her?

She notices a storefront across the street with art pieces on display. Samara walks over to get a better view.

The art is simple but imposing. A large canvas shows a modern-day woman dressed in a business suit and holding a cup of coffee. She smiles without a care in the world, but her body is split in two halves, her insides and organs showing in a clean cut. The art reminds Samara of the cheap heart lockets that friends give each other, two halves meant to be together.

There's no plaque explaining the piece, but the door is open, so Samara enters.

Inside the small gallery, the walls are covered with charcoal sketches of Latinas cut in half. A young girl takes a selfie with her bottom half floating apart from her torso. A mother pushes a stroller, but her hands are not connected to her arms. Broken Latinas everywhere, crying, or smiling, or watching television. About to kiss their lovers, arguing on the street. All disconnected from their bodies.

Samara is overcome with emotion, an ugly truth made visible.

"May I help you?"

The voice startles her. She hadn't noticed the woman sitting in the corner of the gallery, watching her. The woman is in her late thirties. She uses a rag to clean a mug.

"Oh. The door was open and I just thought . . ." Samara says. "I was trying to buy a floral arrangement from across the street."

"They don't open on Saturdays," the woman says.

"Are these yours?" Samara asks. "They're stunning."

The woman approaches her and they both face the pieces. She wears baggy Dickies with a long button-up shirt rolled up at the sleeves and her hair tucked under a bandana. Her neck is covered in silver jewelry and tattoos dot her arms.

"I'm new to Vernon. My name is Samara." She holds out her hand but the woman displays her stained fingers instead.

"Marisa Sol. And yes, these are mine."

Samara falls into the journalist role, asking questions, and Marisa obliges.

"My parents owned and managed buildings here until I took them over." She points outside. "I sold some and kept this one for myself."

"It must be exciting to see this new development happening in Vernon," Samara says. "It's what convinced me to move here from Jersey."

"You think so, huh? It's good for some people," Marisa says. "Rich people trampling over those who are actually from here and polluting our land. Just look at this."

She walks to a table and returns with a stack of business cards, all from real estate agents.

"They can't wait for me to leave so they can build something useless, but I won't ever leave. I'm rooted here. What they're trying to do to me, they're doing to others in the community. Even the church. Trying to erase our history."

"At least people will always need art," Samara says. "Are these for sale? I would love to give one to my boss, Antonio Mota. Have you heard of him? He's from Vernon too."

"The fashion designer," Marisa says with a scoff. "The one that suddenly 'rediscovered' his roots here? Yeah, I know him."

She's dragging Antonio, and maybe even Samara a little bit for working for him. This woman is punchy and Samara kind of likes it. It goes well with the violent surrealism of her work.

"So, how much for this one?" Samara points to a smaller version of the piece on display in the storefront, of the woman in the business suit cut in half. The piece costs way more than Samara expected, but she still buys it.

Marisa wraps the small canvas with brown wrapping paper and ties it with twine. It's even better than a bouquet of flowers.

"Don't believe everything they say to you," Marisa says. "Don't let them fuckers corrupt you."

"Okay, I won't," Samara says, laughing. "Thank you!"

On her walk back to The Murphy, Samara takes another path, wanting to pass by the church the artist mentioned. The church looks ancient, with a tall wooden cross standing erect in front of it. Off to the side a more modern-looking sign listing the service times seems out of place. Next to the church is a carved-out building with scaffolding around it. A sign announcing "Whole Foods Coming Soon" is tied to the gate. She recalls Lake mentioning the future supermarket and how it will change the game for Vernon.

Samara takes a picture of the church and the way the sun's rays highlight the splinters jutting out of the cross like thorns. A woman opens the door, giving Samara a peek inside. The pews are filled with people, an unusual sight on a late Saturday afternoon. The last time Samara was in church was for Abuela Lola.

No, she doesn't want to remember that—anything but that.

"Welcome," the older Latina says, displaying a warm smile. The woman walks down the steps of the church toward her, but Samara doesn't wait. She quickly walks away.

Religion or spirituality has never been her thing; like a parrot, she could recite a couple of verses from Sor Juana Inés de la Cruz, a good trick to use at parties or in an article. She loves the severity of religious garments. Nuns are so sexy in their habits, their skirts stiffly restraining their desires. It's easy to see how Catholicism can be provocative, but religion itself is just a killer of ideas, strict doctrines forcing women to be docile.

If her mother were there she would have forced her to go inside to light a candle. *For Abuela Lola,* she would say.

But she pushes the thought away. She's not going to think about church or funerals or anything that happened back in Jersey. Those memories are buried deep inside, where they will stay.

When she arrives at Antonio's Hancock Park home for dinner, his partner Steven opens the door. Steven works as a trainer and sometimes an actor. His abs are always prominently displayed in daily thirst traps on TikTok, and Samara thinks it's funny what man candy he is—the perfect himbo.

"Hi!" Steven says with such excitement Samara can't help but laugh.

Antonio's austerely designed home is decorated in mostly grays and was recently featured on the pages of *Travel + Leisure*. The only bright colors to be found are in the artwork Antonio collects and displays on the walls. With paintings by the likes of Leonora Carrington and Remedios Varo, Samara can't imagine how much his collection must be worth.

"I got you a little something." Samara gives Antonio the gift. "I thought you might like it."

"Oh, this is gorgeous," he says and hunts for a signature. "Sol . . . I've never heard of her."

"Just a local artist I met today. She was kind of a character. Tattoos up and down her arms, set up in a small gallery on—"

"Did I mention the Spanish artist I want to bring in to use for the runway show?" Antonio asks, interrupting her. He leads her to the dining room and talks about his recent trip to Spain.

"Oh, he sounds amazing!" Samara exclaims before nibbling

on the appetizers being served by Steven. Though Steven set the plates on the table, she can hear him talking to a private chef hidden somewhere in the kitchen.

The rest of the night, Samara is "on." She is funny and charming. She endears herself to Antonio, procuring all the proverbial gold stars. When she leaves, she spots the artwork by Marisa Sol leaning sadly against the entryway's wall.

CHAPTER 10

THE MURPHY IS a short fifteen-minute walk to work, and the plan was always to make the trek every day by foot. It's not even as far a walk as the one she used to take to catch the PATH train. Samara swore she wouldn't be the type of girl who would waste money on car services, but here she is, in a Lyft. She doesn't have the budget for this kind of life, but the lack of sleep is slowly starting to mess with her. Late nights getting home mean even later nights getting to bed only to be awakened at two in the morning by the strange noises and disgusting smells from the slaughterhouse. Ever since she moved into the apartment, the sounds wake her up at the exact same time each night. No matter how many pills or glasses of wine she adds to her sleep routine, it's always broken.

As the car waits for a traffic light to change, Samara turns her head to discover the snout of a pig sniffing the air from inside an idle tractor trailer. In the truck she can see there are so many pigs bumping into each other. One of them manages to push their entire round face through a metal slit.

"Poor pig," Samara says.

The large animal examines her with beady eyes. She remembers a time when everyone in the industry wanted a pet pig. Samara traveled to upstate New York once to interview a former model-slash-beauty skin guru. The photographer drove them both up to the woman's sprawling farmhouse. They took so many pictures of the tall model with flowing red wavy hair walking her pig through town. Mathilda was the name of the animal, and Samara kept thinking about how much she craved a medianoche sandwich and how ridiculous the woman seemed to her in high heels, walking a pig who wore a hat that cost more than Samara's whole outfit.

"Are you and your friends keeping me up at night?" Samara asks. The pig points its snout up to the cloudy sky. She doesn't want to think about the animal's inevitable demise.

The light changes and the truck veers left while her driver continues forward.

A little later, settled in her office, Samara adjusts the intricate braided leather harness she wore to toughen up her diaphanous maxi dress. She leaves her door open so she can hear the sewing machines while she takes another stab at drafting the fashion show's theme statement. Once approved, the one-pager will be shared company-wide so that everyone will be aware of the concept Antonio wants his fashion show to convey. Every campaign, advertisement, press talking point—everything will be pulled from Samara's writing.

On her desk are several reference books, specific titles Antonio mentioned to her, others she's looked up herself: *Inventing the Dream: California Through the Progressive Era*. *We Are the Land*. *Testimonios: Early California Through the Eyes of Women, 1815–*

1848. Poetry by Henri Coulette and Wanda Coleman. Joan Didion essays. This is just the beginning of the research, and Samara loves this part. Learning about California and cobbling together a history of Vernon along the way. She takes extensive notes and spends her morning collecting the right words for the theme.

The one-pager is due by the end of December, which is not too bad, but her time is taken up by other responsibilities. She oversees the tone of campaigns, press releases, and product descriptions, making sure Antonio's voice is consistent throughout. Then there are meetings about new products, reports to write on social media engagement metrics, potential celebrity ambassadors, and the web redesign that he's adamant be done before the show.

"Who wrote this? This isn't how I sound at all!" Antonio screeches from the middle of the workroom. "Samara!"

She steps into the Design Department. Everyone looks down, focusing on their own work. No one wants to be blamed.

"Samara, what is this?" He flings a paper at a table with disgust. Lisa and the intern walk over, looking at the printout like some strange new discovery, even though it's Lisa's words on the page. The marketing copy, printed out for Antonio to read, is meant to run across the company's social media platforms.

"I don't understand what any of you are doing!" He suddenly slaps the table, causing his workers to jump—but not Samara. She approaches the paper like a doctor examining a dying patient with compassion and purpose.

"Let me take a look . . . Oh, I see it now. We're not hitting the marketing points," Samara says. She's learned to pick up the keywords that are always driving Antonio's work. "These sentences aren't conveying what you're about. They're not describing that intersection of beauty and brutality."

He shakes his head angrily and Samara places her hand atop his. "Let me rework this right now."

Samara pulls out a red pen and drags lines through paragraphs so loudly and so hard she almost rips the paper while Lisa bristles beside her. It's Lisa's words being deleted, even after being approved by most of the departments.

"We'll have a new version for you in an hour," Samara says. An annoyed Antonio dismisses them. Samara walks with Lisa back to their space.

"The copy was fine last time he saw it," Lisa mutters.

"Don't take it personally. He's just feeling the pressure. It's on us to mind read and make sure it's perfect."

Lisa slumps at her desk, angrily typing away.

"Let me pick us up a snack so we can work through it together for the next hour. Okay?" Samara offers.

Anyone else would send the intern to get them some provisions, but she needs a break. Antonio's outbursts are increasing in number, and each incident worse than the last. It's still only December—what will he be like next month as the date for the show draws nearer?

There's a food truck always stationed nearby where workers from the factories can converge. A lot of Samara's co-workers go there too, because it's easier than waiting for an expensive salad to be delivered.

A trio of Latinas huddle together waiting for their orders. The sleeves on their long white jackets are rolled up with the Consuelo's Farmhouse logo neatly sewn on the chest. They seem so young, no more than eighteen, if that. What is it like to work in a slaughterhouse? How the stink must stick to their skin. One of the workers says hello and Samara smiles back.

It would be great to stage a photo shoot with these workers placed alongside the models. Maybe have a couple of them wearing Mota. No one really knowing who is the working model and who isn't. They can shoot it in The Saprophyte or perhaps even at the Farmhouse. A kind of high-low, death-and-life feel. Antonio would love it. She'll bring it up to him after he's cooled off. Get him to focus on the photo shoot instead of how he thinks his employees are failing him.

Samara concentrates on the food offerings, mouthing the names of the dishes to herself and thinking through what might be the healthiest choice. A couple of workers order before her in their steady Spanish. When it's Samara's turn, she asks for a quesadilla with only a little cheese. The food truck owner doesn't understand, and Samara feels her face burning up.

"¿Sin queso?" she asks.

"¿Quieres una quesadilla sin queso?" The vendor shakes her head, confused. There's a long line and Samara's adding to the delay.

"That's not what I meant." She gets flustered. "Umm. Cómo se dice . . ."

"Lupe, relaja con el queso para la señorita. Solo un poco, ¿eh?"

Samara faces the man speaking for her. He has a full white beard contrasting with closely shorn dark hair in the style Ricky Martin debuted a year ago. Not many men can pull off the look, but this man can. He wears a crisp button-up shirt with a slim, Burberry suit. Very slick.

"Thank you," she says to him.

"Por supuesto."

The way he speaks Spanish . . . it's old-school, respectful, with a glint of mischief. Or maybe Samara is reading more into the exchange than what it really was: just a random guy who felt sorry for the gringa. He orders for himself and Samara tries to keep to a minimum the number of times she looks at him.

The man talks to the young workers from Consuelo's. They

giggle and return his Spanish with hints of honey. Samara's jealous of how smoothly they communicate and how she still stumbles over the simplest of phrases. She pulls out her phone and inconspicuously snaps a photo of the group. She fools herself into thinking the picture is to show Antonio a reference for the possible shoot.

"Buen provecho," he says when she picks up her order. She sashays away, shaking her ass more than usual, until a blast of toxic odor from the slaughterhouse stops her dead in her tracks. She coughs from the stench, the smell filling up her lungs.

Samara has learned to time her walks outside of the office to avoid the Vernon perfume, but Antonio's tantrum messed her up. The odorous onslaught is relentless.

"Ten cuidado."

A woman's voice floats in from somewhere. The urgent warning, a whisper.

Samara turns to locate the whisperer but she can't pinpoint it. The factory workers are too immersed in their conversation with the fine-looking man. They're not paying attention to Samara or even seeming to notice the smell. Instead, they laugh at his jokes while Samara holds her breath to keep from throwing up.

By the time she drops off the food at Lisa's desk, she no longer feels like eating.

CHAPTER 11

It's been more than two weeks since she's spoken to her family, aside from the occasional text. This is the longest Samara has gone avoiding them, but she can't push it off any longer. Every text Samara gets from her mother is followed by a call. The insistent ringing feels like her mother is yelling at her. That it's FaceTime makes it all the more violent, but this time Samara is ready. She's managed to move across the States without breaking down, without asking them for help. Antonio loves her. The workers do too—minus Dolores, but even the seamstress will eventually come around. Besides, Samara has to break the news to her parents that she will not be coming home for the holidays.

Before answering the call, Samara positions the phone so that the beautiful sunny blue sky is behind her.

"Mami came to me in a dream," her mother says as soon as she appears on the screen, only showing her eyes and forehead. It doesn't matter how many times Samara explains to her family where exactly to situate their faces; they always appear on FaceTime with their heads chopped off or their thumbs blocking the camera.

The mention of her grandmother stings. Abuela hasn't appeared to Samara in her dreams at all since her death, but according to her mother, she's been making house calls to everyone else in the family—not just her mother, but her cousins and even the guy who used to pack her groceries. How is it that Abuela Lola is sending spiritual signals to everyone but her?

"She did?" Samara asks, trying to mask her disappointment. "What did Abuela Lola say?"

"In the dream, she kept looking for you all over the house, and when I told her you were gone, she started to cry."

Samara wants to hang up, but she also wants to hear more. She misses her grandmother so much. Although Samara grew up in a Catholic home, her family is no stranger to ancestors offering advice from the other side. Samara thought for sure her grandmother would have appeared to her by now, guiding her like she always did, especially after what happened.

"Maybe that was *you* crying in the dream and not Abuela Lola," Samara says, but her mother shakes her head.

"This is all a misunderstanding. Tú sabes cómo es la familia. You and mami were always confusing what people say," her mother says. "Siempre peleándose con los demás. But we're family."

Samara doesn't want to go over what happened, what was said, or how Abuela Lola is no longer there to help her explain.

"Please stop," she says. "Please stop talking or I'm going to hang up."

"This is a sign from mami to come home. You don't have to be so far away."

Her mother isn't listening even as Samara pleads with her.

"Your cousins are worried about you. Even your cousin Benjy was—"

"I have to go. No, I'm not talking about this." Samara hangs up.

Her hands are shaking. She feels like her head is being slowly immersed in water, cutting off her breathing. She needs to get out of here. As Samara searches for her house keys, her phone rings and rings. Samara sends the call to voicemail.

Okay, I promise. No more talking. Only you talk, reads the text from her mother.

Samara gives herself a few minutes. She splashes cold water on her face and waits until her pulse is no longer plucking like a taut rubber band ready to snap. She grabs a bottle of the wine she drinks every night before sleeping and pours herself a glass.

Her relationship with her mother has always been this way, but at least when Abuela Lola was around, there was a buffer between them. Why doesn't her grandmother speak to her in her dreams instead of leaving her to crave these tiny morsels her mother shares? And somehow, her mother still finds a way to guilt her for leaving Jersey through these visions. But her mother will not win. Samara left. It's a done deal.

"Do you want to see the apartment?" Samara asks when her mother answers her call.

"Pues claro." Her mother's lips are painted her usual orange-red, and she's wearing a slight hint of eyeshadow. *Se presentan* is what they say about the Martín women. They always looked so put together, like the glossy images in the fashion magazines.

Samara inhales deeply and then gives a tour of her place.

"Ah, qué lindo. ¿Pero no hay puertas?"

"It's a studio, Mom. An open space," she says. "And this is the kitchen."

"Tan chiquito. How can you cook there?"

"I can cook fine."

"¿Y el trabajo?"

Finally, something Samara's been wanting to share. "It's great. Everyone is nice, especially Antonio," she says. "This is what I've been wanting to do, to write only about fashion. No more celebrity interviews. No more chasing after work. A steady check. I'm really happy."

"¡Qué bueno! We want you to be happy. That's all we ever wanted," she says. "Now tell me more about the city you think is better than your own home and I'll tell you what happened to Chucha the other day."

Her mother gives her the lowdown on neighborhood drama, who is doing what to whom. Samara nurses her drink, not really paying attention, her mother's sentences floating in and out.

"I haven't been sleeping." Samara is surprised by her own confession because it comes out of nowhere. She blames the glass of wine and her mother's chatter. Her mother stops wiping the countertop. They're both in their respective kitchens and that gives Samara a bit of solace.

"It's probably the air. Los Angeles has dirty air," her mother says. "Or the water. Are you using a Brita?"

"The water? What does the water have to do with my sleep?"

"You've never liked drinking water." Her mother goes on about Samara's lack of hydration and how she preferred orange juice ever since she was a little girl. Abuela Lola always had a large glass of OJ for her every morning. *It helps you grow,* she would say, and it didn't matter that when she was far into adulthood, Samara still accepted the glass of juice with its high sugar content as a sweet morning blessing from her grandmother.

Samara clutches the glass of wine tight, gulps down the remains, and pours another.

"What's happening?" her mother asks.

She inhales deeply, already regretting this conversation, but there's a longing for any insight her mother might be able to give her about her insomnia. She wants to tell her mother about the unusual noises she hears every night, but there's a fine line between admitting her sleep problems and exploring that maybe something deeper is off. It's not that she doesn't want to worry her mother, it's just she doesn't want her to win, her predictions about the move being proven true by these unexplained disturbances. Her mother believing that Samara must be at fault here. It's not the water or the dirty air. It's Samara's weak life choices. And yet, she's the one who brought it up, so she proceeds reluctantly.

"Every night I wake up at two in the morning to weird noises."

"Noises?"

"Yes," she says. "It sounds like someone crying or whimpering. I don't know. And sometimes it sounds like rustling, like something trying to break free from a trap."

"Those are rats. You should talk to the building manager about it," her mother says. "Don't leave food out in the open. Clean up after yourself. Are you cleaning the kitchen?"

Samara was dumb to think her mother might actually help in any way. Instead she's just supplying her with more ammunition—more reasons why Samara should give up and come home.

"Okay, Mom. I'll talk to the manager about it," she says, all of a sudden feeling exhausted. "I'll call you next week."

"You'll be here for Christmas, right? The family is expecting you."

"No, can't," Samara says. "I'm spending the holidays here. I have to work."

"Work? Nobody works during Christmas!" her mother replies. "What about the family? What will I tell them?"

"Don't make me feel bad because I'm doing what you've raised me to do," she says. "I need to go."

"Where are you going?" her mother asks. Samara's anxiety rises.

"I'm going to talk to the manager about the rats," she says. "I'll call you next week. Te quiero, bye."

Samara rides the empty elevator down.

"How can I help you?" Raul asks when she approaches.

"I think there are rats behind the walls of my apartment," she says. "I keep hearing them every night."

"I'll have maintenance send someone over to check that," Raul says. "It's an old building, like a lot of the buildings here in Vernon. It's full of weird creaks, old pipes."

"The sound I'm hearing is rustling, like a rodent trying to get in," she says. "Not an old water pipe heating up."

"Maybe it's the ghosts," he says, teasing. "They say Vernon is haunted."

"Haunted? And what do you say?" Samara asks. "You believe that?"

"Me? I'm not paid to believe. I'm paid to mind my business," he says. "We'll get maintenance to your place later this evening."

"I don't have time for ghosts or rats or old pipes," Samara says. "I just want quiet. Thanks, Raul."

When she presses the elevator button to go back up to her floor, Samara thinks of how Abuela Lola appears in other people's dreams. The only haunting she wants is one from her grandmother telling her that she's doing a good job.

—

At two in the morning, the sound of a low grunt enters Samara's apartment like a curse, reminding her that sleep will not come. As on previous nights, Samara groggily gets up and walks to the window, searching to connect the noise to someone or something, only to be met with darkness.

"Please, shut up," she says, but the sound persists.

Her thoughts drift to the funeral. The open casket and all those tears. Soon she recalls what happened after the service.

She doesn't want to go there. To stop that day of death from manifesting itself again in her mind, Samara opens another bottle of wine. She buries the dark event by finishing the bottle, and then opening another. Not until the walls of the apartment start to slowly spin and the animal grunts begin to fade to the background does she lay her head down on the pillow.

CHAPTER 12

SAMARA LOVES TO work in the archives. The room has become her second office, a place she can take a temporary breather from work drama. No Antonio screaming her name with urgency, every small thing a catastrophe to be fixed by her. Alone, she can write and be inspired by the clothes themselves. And play.

She pulls out a beaded sleeveless garment with a fringed skirt. The gown is meant to depict the horrors of war, to make the wearer appear to be bleeding. She undresses, locates the zipper, and climbs in. As Samara adjusts the skirt, something pokes her. A needle perhaps, or a clothing tag documenting its placement in Antonio's timeline. She tugs at the fabric and tries to find the culprit.

"Ouch."

Samara quickly takes the dress off to find a long scratch on her right hip. A bubble of blood emerges. Samara presses down on the injury with her thumb. In her underwear, she flips the garment inside out, looking for any loose pins. Goose bumps cover her bare legs. Samara walks under the ceiling's light fixture to take a closer look.

There it is. A lone pin sticks out, but there's something else. Inside the gown Samara finds a black thread sewn along a seam. A word is stitched with a letter *P* prominent. She starts to decipher the other letters, trying to guess what word they form.

"Piedad," she says loudly. The letters are uneven and childlike, stitched by someone with little skill. The thread on the stitches is definitely not the same one used on the rest of the gown. She repeats the name again. "Piedad."

Antonio has never mentioned a Piedad when he talks about his family history. It's only ever been about Ramona and the fierce warrior figure she was. Samara pulls another dress from the same period. It takes her a while but finally, she locates the name again. *Piedad*. She pulls out another blouse and there it is, the name hidden under a pocket. And in a pair of slacks. And a skirt. Antonio is going to have a fit when he finds out how his archives are being ruined. Who did this?

"Someone's getting fucked," she says.

As she puts her clothes back on, she remembers how she was the last person to visit the archives last night. She'd examined some of the same pieces and found nothing wrong with the clothes then. Thinking it through, the only workers who would have had the opportunity to slip into the archive and do this without being seen would be the seamstresses.

Samara opens the red door and stares out to the women hunched over their sewing machines. Half of them are working on fulfilling current orders. Others concentrate on samples Antonio wants made for the February show. There's no way Samara will take the blame for destroying the archives. No, this will not land in her lap, but she must proceed delicately. She can't just start accusing her co-workers.

Samara leaves the Library and returns to her office to think through her options. While answering emails, she considers what course of action to take. Should she go straight to Antonio or confront the seamstresses first? Samara takes her chances on the latter.

"Excuse me, Dolores. I want to show you something," she says. "Can you come with me?"

Although Samara can clearly see her reluctance, Dolores gets up and drapes her office sweater around her shoulders before following her back to the Library.

The seamstress glances over at the turn-of-the-century-style metal-and-wood clock on the wall and then back to Samara. This is Dolores's warning to be quick.

Samara grabs the red-beaded gown and shows it to Dolores. "When was this name sewn into the dress?"

"I don't know what you're talking about," the seamstress says after a slight pause.

"What do you mean? The name. It's right there."

"There's nothing there." Dolores nudges the dress back to her.

"What?" Samara searches the garment. Dolores is right. The name is gone. She returns to the rack and pulls another dress and a blouse, the same ones from before. Each design is missing the name sewn into the fabric.

"Wait a minute. It was just there. The name Piedad handsewn into the clothes. I saw it." Samara searches through the other racks, trying to prove her point. Dolores just stands there.

The seamstress pulls up her reading glasses hanging around her neck and takes a closer look. "No. There is nothing wrong with these clothes," she says.

"Oh hell no," Samara mutters. She's not losing her mind. She saw it. They must have taken the stitches out somehow. Samara's face reddens but she continues to search for the name Piedad stitched in along the seams. She makes a mess while Dolores watches. "Was it one of your workers? Did you have them remove the stitches?"

Dolores clucks her tongue. "None of my girls have access to the archives. I have a key. Antonio has a key. And now you."

Samara's not having it.

"Dolores, I know you think I'm dense, but I'm not. The clothes all had the name Piedad. I saw it with my own eyes."

The woman puckers her lips. Flecks of dried pink lipstick flake off. Dolores sighs, a sound of disappointment, or perhaps of something more.

"There's no name on there now, is there?" she asks. Dolores gently takes the skirt Samara's clutching too tightly and moves under the ceiling lamp. "I don't see it. Do you?"

Samara looks around the room and the chaos she just inflicted upon it. Clothes strewn everywhere. She doesn't know what to think. Did she make it up? No, she was standing in this very room not even an hour ago, staring at the name. She was, wasn't she?

"I . . . um. I'm sorry, Dolores," Samara says, confused.

Dolores turns and pauses by the door. She examines Samara intensely. "Maybe you're working too hard," she says before leaving.

Samara doesn't understand what just happened. Where did the names go?

Lisa pokes her head in and warns her she's late to a meeting. And with that, a defeated Samara snaps out of the murkiness of her mind.

"Is everything okay?" Lisa asks while helping Samara place the garments back.

"Someone's playing games with me," she says. "But I am not playing."

Lisa laughs uneasily.

"Never mind me, I'm just thinking out loud," Samara cheerfully says, trying to even out her angry tone. She doesn't need Lisa or anyone else wondering what's going on. "Thank you so much for helping me get this room back in order."

Samara spends her time at the meeting going over what happened, getting more and more angry.

They're trying to trip me up, Samara thinks, *but I'm not going to fall.*

An idea starts to form, or at least the beginning stages of an idea. She nurtures it, all the while thinking: *Who the fuck is Piedad?*

CHAPTER 13

LATER THAT DAY, Samara decides to put her thought in motion. There's an order to the family lunch, a ranking as to where people are to be seated. The hierarchy was set way before Samara started working there. She accepts the order because she's been consistently seated next to Antonio and that's what counts. Her job is to never lose that spot. But Samara decides to manipulate the family lunch formula. Even before she takes her seat next to Tommy, Samara sets her intention.

"Rosa, come sit by us," she says, waving the seamstress in.

"I'm fine, I should sit here." Rosa is apologetic, but Samara is going to insist.

"Rosa, we have more than enough room for you," she says. "Don't worry, we don't bite."

Samara can tell Rosa wants to join the fortunate ones at Antonio's table. She can also see how much her actions bother Dolores.

"What are you doing?" Tommy asks.

"Isn't this a family lunch?" Samara asks. "I'm just trying to get to know everyone."

Tommy shakes his head.

"Apparently Samara is choosing chaos today. The seamstresses always sit together," Alex says. "You don't want to tangle with Dolores."

"I'm not worried about it," Samara says. The clothes in the archives were screwed with and Dolores knows it. But her gaslighting Samara is a sign for her to wake up. She doesn't care how long Dolores has worked for Antonio or how important she is to him. Samara won't be intimidated by anyone, not when it comes to this job.

"Come here," Samara says firmly. She ignores the glare being directed at her by Dolores and the other seamstresses. "Sit."

A timid Rosa walks over to them. The scowl from Dolores is immediate.

When Lake places Antonio's usual fancy salad on the table, she's surprised by the new seating arrangement.

"Oh hi, Rosa!" she says.

"Rosa is joining the wild ones today," Samara says. "Did you know she's interested in modeling and maybe assisting in styling? Isn't that great?"

"That's good to know," Lake says. "Antonio loves when people show initiative. We should talk later. You never know what might come up."

"But what will Dolores say?" Alex teases.

"Rosa is at a crossroads where either she walks toward the devil or gets left behind with the angels," Samara says. "Which will she choose?"

Samara enjoys witnessing her social strategy in action. Dolores continues to shoot intense looks at them. Rosa seems uncomfortable, but like a smart, ambitious woman, she pulls up the collar of her blouse to conceal the cross that rests near her collarbone.

Soon Antonio sits at the head of the table. He doesn't even bat an eye over the sudden musical chairs. None of it matters so long as he's still the sun and everyone else just orbits around him.

"Samara, how's the one-pager coming along?" he asks. "When will I see something from you?"

"I'll definitely have something for you early next week. It's been so much fun going through the archives and seeing all the beautiful garments you've created throughout the years," she says. "Is it true Dolores worked on most of them?"

He takes a bite from his salad. "Almost all of them. Dolores was with me from the very beginning in my small studio apartment, working right beside me."

"I remember you mentioning something about having pictures of her when she was young," Samara says. "I would love to see them."

The designer takes out his tablet and scrolls through albums until he finds the image of a girl about eighteen years old. Dolores has beautiful cascading curls and wears a form-fitting wiggle dress with her cleavage leading her pose. There's something so sexual in the way she holds the side of her waist and leans forward that Samara finds it hard to believe this was once Dolores. The woman she works with is severe and unyielding like the needles in her pincushion. In the photo, her mouth was caught mid-laugh and so wide open that Samara can practically see the back of her teeth. This Dolores is free and uninhibited.

"She was gorgeous," Samara says.

"Yes. She's always had this guarded beauty about her."

"She doesn't seem so guarded in this photo."

Rosa shifts in her seat, and Samara finds her unease thrilling.

"I've always been fascinated by constraint and unbridled sensuality. Think of the Victorian era," Antonio says. "How a hint of an ankle can become provocative. Dolores is a reminder of that. Of a sexuality that changes as we grow older. You might see a serious woman, but I still see her like this."

Samara doesn't see Dolores like that at all. Instead, she sees someone who is out to sabotage her standing with Antonio.

"What you're saying right now is so inspiring. With all my time spent in the archives, I've been thinking so much about your history and The Ramona dress," she says. "Why don't we do a quick photo shoot with it? The location should be here in Vernon, right at The Saprophyte, and next door at the slaughterhouse."

"Oh no, not Consuelo's," Alex interrupts while Antonio pushes his salad to the side. Antonio is not interested in hearing anything about Consuelo's, but Samara presses on.

"Listen, Antonio, you've built your legacy on subverting the norm," Samara continues. "Consuelo's is part of Vernon history, and you should reclaim it by connecting its horror with beauty. Remember when you used to do everything on your own, without a timetable or judgments? This is what the industry has to be reminded of: how much of a master you are at eliminating the lines."

"But Consuelo's?" Tommy asks, raising his eyebrows.

"We won't use models. Instead we'll use workers, like Rosa here. Even Dolores can be in it. Meat hooks dangling, blood everywhere, and The Ramona in the middle of it," she says. "Consider it a preview of what they'll be seeing in February."

"Hmmm, a preview . . ." Antonio considers what she says.

"I'm sure we can do something great," Samara adds.

The longer Samara gasses Antonio about his legacy, the

more the designer gets into the idea. Everyone warned her never to mention the slaughterhouse, but here she is, convincing her boss to shoot there. Getting Rosa to sit by them was the first step in her plan and it's working, so Samara takes it further.

"There's something else I wanted to mention. It's not a big deal, but I saw something in the archives this morning, something really weird," she says. "There was a name sewn into the seams of a few of the clothes. It's gone now but is there a reason why someone would do that? The only people who arrive early at work are Dolores and the seamstresses. Why would she do that to the clothes?"

"Dolores would never do that," Antonio says. "Never."

"I don't mean to say she would, but I did see this name sewn in the clothes, and the only people who might have gotten to the archives this morning are the seamstresses. Since she gets here first, Dolores would have seen something and—"

"No!"

The table goes quiet. Samara has finally stepped over the line.

"I wasn't accusing her of anything," she tries to retract, but it's too late. Antonio is fuming.

"Dolores would never do that to the pieces in the archives. *Never.*"

"I just thought it was strange. I wasn't accusing anyone." The more she tries to explain herself, the further away Antonio becomes. She's losing her place in the designer's benevolent glow.

"Dolores is the one person in this whole company who only thinks of protecting me," he says. "The next time you see something that's off, tell Lake or anyone else. Don't assume you know anything."

Samara looks around the table. No one is coming to her rescue. They're all too busy eating their lunches, except for Rosa. Her big brown eyes are filled with anxiety.

"Antonio, you have a call with the distributors at two," Lake says, saving Samara from fumbling even more. With that reminder, Antonio leaves and Samara must contend with the whole room, including the men in the pictures, pointing accusatory fingers at her.

Lunch is soon over. When Dolores passes their table, she taps on Rosa's shoulder and without hesitation, Rosa follows the others back to the workroom.

There's a hint of glee emanating from her co-workers, excited by how the favored child has been taken down a notch.

"Gooble gobble, one of us," Tommy says. "We accept her, one of us."

Samara laughs along with him, pretending everything is fine.

CHAPTER 14

"BECAUSE YOU HAVEN'T been here as long, a word of advice," Alex says with attitude, tossing her blond highlights around. "It's probably best to clear big projects with me before presenting them to Antonio so my team isn't blindsided."

Since she started working, it's been nothing but a lovefest, but last Friday's family lunch began Samara's descent. Since returning to work after having the day off for Christmas, Samara feels like she's been walking around with a scarlet letter on her back. She needs the photo shoot to be a win, to erase the bad taste she left with Antonio when she tried to fuck Dolores over.

"Sure, I'll remember next time," she says to appease Alex. "What do we have to do to make this happen? Do you have an in with Consuelo's?"

"We tried this idea a couple of years ago," she says. "It's not possible for us to shoot at the factory, which means we'll have to replicate it here somehow. And it's the holidays. We're not going to be able to pull this off on such short notice."

"What if we shoot in front of it? I'm sure they wouldn't mind the exposure."

Alex laughs bitterly. "Consuelo's Farmhouse doesn't need exposure from a fashion house."

"Look, we can recruit a couple of workers from Consuelo's. They would be perfect."

"We've been through this before."

No matter what Samara says, Alex's team refuses to give an inch. Alex wants to prove a point. Maybe she's finally over how Antonio was going to Samara for advice on the smallest things. Thankfully, the designer already approved the idea. Samara will see it through even if she has to do it herself.

"Hello!" A boisterous voice breaks the tension by knocking at the door. "Am I late to the meeting?"

Then enters the man Samara saw a few weeks ago at the food truck with the sexy vibe. He's wearing a tan, slim-fitted Tom Ford suit with brown suede loafers and a wool sweater. The color nicely offsets his dark tousled hair, giving his whole style a relaxed look, like he's not trying hard at all. Alex drops her bitch face and greets him with a warm embrace.

"Brandon, you came just in time," she says.

He gives everyone a hug until he stops at Samara.

"This is Samara Martín, our new global brand director," Alex says.

"Nice to meet you." Recognition crosses between them.

"Likewise, Samara," he says, rolling the *r* in her name. "I'm Brandon Hernandez and I come bearing gifts."

He presents her with a box of pastries.

"You know we don't eat carbs here," Alex says.

Brandon opens the pink box and pulls out napkins and small plates. "You might not, but Lake and the interns and everyone else who is smart will. Real World Donuts is about to open their first California outpost right here in Vernon."

RWD is the latest bakery craze in New York. Lines out the door with people trying to get a taste of the extra-rich donuts.

"I'm helping them get the word out." He picks one of the donuts and offers it to her. Unlike Alex, she takes it.

"Brandon is practically the mayor of Vernon," Lisa says. "He knows everyone."

He brushes off the comment. "Just a venture capitalist involved in a little bit of everything, like donuts. What do you think? Pretty good? I got them to forgo downtown rents and open a café a street over. I'll make sure Antonio's employees get free donuts—I mean coffee."

"So, Brandon, do you have any good contacts with Consuelo's Farmhouse?" Samara asks.

He digs in his pocket, pulls out a card and a pen. "Here's my personal number. Text me and I'll try my best to help you, Señorita Martín," he says. "Now, is your boss in and does he need a donut?"

"I'd say he needs at least two," Alex says.

"Say no more." After neatly plating two donuts, he leaves. The unexpected interruption by the charming Brandon does the trick. Alex's annoyed exterior disappears.

"So who is he?" Samara asks, taking another bite from the glorious treat.

"An old friend of Antonio's," she says, finally submitting to the donut temptation. "I think they graduated from the same private school but like, twenty years apart."

Samara recalls an interview where Antonio stated he attended public schools in New York and how his family never had much money. Another fabricated detail to add to his tale of a tortured artist. That no one has ever checked his background is another indication that people believe what they want to believe.

"Do you think he can really help with the photo shoot?" Samara asks. Her sticky fingers delicately hold the edges of the business card.

"If he likes you, he will," Alex says.

"Well, let's hold off on booking the location and do a quick casting here," Samara says. "We can bribe the workers to do the photo shoot with these donuts. C'mon, it'll be fun."

Maybe it's the sugar from the pastries or Brandon's sudden appearance, but Alex and her team let go of Samara's pariah status. For the rest of the day, Samara feels hopeful again.

Later in her apartment, she checks her phone. Brandon still hasn't responded to her earlier text and she can't help but write him off as another Hollywood fake. It's been almost a month since she's moved to California and she hasn't really met anyone interesting enough to fuck. Drinks with her co-workers only led to meeting men who were ineligible—mostly beautiful model friends of Tommy's or actors-slash-screenwriters-slash-directors. She's had no exciting dick news to relay back to Angie, who always seems to have a new lover in the rotation every time they talk, which has admittedly been less and less lately.

To stop herself from obsessing over how Brandon hasn't texted her back even though he'd clearly read her message, she prepares herself a home-cooked meal of yuca con mojo and ropa vieja. She's been avoiding cooking Cuban food because the act reminds her of Abuela Lola and the times they spent in the kitchen. During those times, her grandmother would recall stories of how suitors would serenade her with beautiful boleros.

She spurned them all until she met Abuelo Alfonso at the factory.

"He was very serious," Abuela Lola said. She never talked about any love or passion she felt for him, only about how well Abuelo Alfonso provided for her.

Samara eats her meal with music playing. Her apartment is small but it's all *hers*. Her things. Her furniture. Her kitchen table. She opens a bottle of wine.

Abuela Lola would be so proud of what I've done, she thinks. *How far I've come.*

Samara refills the glass. She ignores how much more she drinks now that she lives alone. It's hard to gauge if she's drinking too much, especially since her friends are not there to join her. Isn't this how white people do it? Wine with meals like a fancy bitch. Samara ends up polishing off the bottle and falls asleep on the sofa.

The vibration from an incoming text on her phone wakes her. Her grogginess makes her unsure of whether she's drunk or dreaming. With eyes half-open, she manages to make it to the bathroom without bumping into anything. She forgot to take off her makeup and a black-and-red streak underneath her eye appears like a bruise. Her phone continues to buzz. Samara walks toward the sound, locating her phone on the floor where she dropped it. She stands by the open window.

A text from Brandon with the name of a contact at Consuelo's.

I hope this helps and that we connect again soon. Reach out if you're craving more donuts.

Her fingers hover over the phone. She wants to reply but she won't. It's two in the morning.

A familiar snuffling sound floats in from outside, the same noise she's heard every night at this hour. And like clockwork,

Samara does what she always does: She stares out into the empty Vernon streets in search of an answer. This time, she sees something. It's dark but eventually the silhouette comes into view under the streetlamp. The night has formed a figure.

A woman walks in the middle of the street. She wears a lace dress, cream-colored, loose-fitting and dated. The woman appears injured, her body slightly hunched over with both her arms across her stomach holding it in pain. Her hair is long and tangled, maybe even wet. The woman stops right underneath Samara's window. Samara strains her neck to get a better look. The woman doubles over in agony.

"Hey!" she yells, pounding on her window to get her attention. "Hey, are you okay?"

Slowly, the woman raises her arms above her head. The hands are covered in what appears to be blood. Red streaks drip down her chest.

"Oh my god!" Samara picks up the house phone and dials zero to connect with the doorman.

"How may I help you, Ms. Martín?" Raul's voice sounds hoarse, tired.

"There's a woman outside bleeding! Right out front. Call an ambulance!"

"Hello, Ms. Martín? Hello? It's hard to hear you." An animalistic grunt emits from the receiver. Samara drops the phone, grabs her keys, and races to the elevator. When she reaches the lobby, Raul stares at her, confused.

"She's right there. A woman. She's bleeding!"

Raul runs outside with her, taking out his walkie-talkie to connect with 911. Samara leads the way, her heart pounding.

But when she reaches the location where she saw the bleeding woman, there's no one there. Not a trace of blood or anything. Just an empty street.

"Hello!" Samara yells out. "We can help you!"

Raul jogs farther down for signs of the missing woman but soon returns.

"There's no one here," he says. "Are you sure you saw someone?"

"I . . . I'm sure I saw her. She was right there. I think . . ." she says. Samara rubs her temples.

"I'm sorry," she says, feeling foolish.

They slowly walk back to the building. When Raul holds the door open for her, Samara doesn't meet his eyes.

"Good night, Ms. Martín. Get some rest," he says gently, like a concerned father. Samara nods her head, unsure of what she actually saw. The stress of the photo shoot must already be getting to her. It has her seeing things. She needs to calm down and stop projecting her anxiety outward.

Samara takes a few deep breaths until she settles her racing heart.

CHAPTER 15

Antonio is not impressed by the models, and it's just a matter of time before he explodes. Lake replaces his already-cold mug of tea with a new one, then she quietly slips away. Samara only wishes she had that option.

"This isn't what I want," Antonio says, shuffling the Polaroids like a bad deck of cards.

Brandon came through with the connection to Consuelo's. In less than a week, they were able to secure a photo shoot on the factory's property, although not inside, food regulations being what they are. It was a complete hustle to get everything ready. A lot of tempers flared and popped off, but everyone pulled through. Samara's idea was to intersperse real workers from the factory with models, so they gathered some Polaroids of those who'd volunteered to appear in the shoot in exchange for clothes. All Antonio has to do is look at the Polaroids and approve which factory employees he'd like in the shoot.

The shoot should have begun two hours ago.

"These girls look like they belong in *Vanidades,*" Antonio says. "Where's the edge? You had days to figure this out."

Samara exchanges a look with Alex. They've both been up since six in the morning, getting everything ready. Heavy makeup does nothing to conceal the bags under Samara's eyes. And she can't shake the vision of the woman with bleeding hands no matter how hard she focuses on work, or how many drinks she consumes at night to help her forget.

"There are others," Samara says. She searches through the batches of Polaroids. "What about her?"

Antonio swats the photo away, more proof that his love for her is dead. If this shoot doesn't move forward, she'll be the one to bear the brunt of its failure.

"This is so cliché. Shooting at a slaughterhouse," Antonio says. "It's nothing new. Nothing original."

Rosa walks into the workroom wearing a tight-fitting black dress with a restraining bodice made of red plastic. The bodice fits her so tightly she can barely breathe. Antonio walks over to her and roughly adjusts the skirt, which is embellished with embroidered thorns. With her long dark hair slicked back into a bun and deep red lips, she looks like a dominatrix. Rosa is exactly what Antonio is looking for and for a second, he seems content, but it doesn't last.

"What else do you have?" he asks.

"I think with Rosa, we should be able to get some good shots," Samara says. The selection of factory workers from Consuelo's was very limited. Not many people were willing to leave their shifts, even when their boss said the volunteers would still be paid their normal rate. And of those few to do it, most weren't striking enough. The male workers were easier to cast:

They wouldn't be dressed in Antonio's clothes but would just stand in their uniforms alongside the models like props. But the women are meant to wear Antonio's designs, and finding the right model to pose in The Ramona became the biggest challenge of all.

"If we style Rosa, she can be our Ramona. And Rosa is from Vernon—the press will love that."

"No, she doesn't have *that* quality at all," Antonio says. "I want something else. Show me something. Anything!"

It seems like soothing Antonio's doubts is all Samara does these days. "Let's just try it. We'll shoot Rosa in this look first and then change her into The Ramona." Alex and Lisa chime in with how it's a great idea. In fact, everyone's in agreement, sounding like parrots, all trying to salvage the hard work they've done.

"Just fix this! I'm surrounded by fucking idiots!" Antonio flings his mug against a wall. The whole room freezes. Her coworkers know exactly how to react—eyes dropping to the floor, waiting for Antonio's anger to subside—but not Samara.

"You don't have to talk to me like that," she blurts out, forgetting who she's talking to.

Tommy pops his head up from behind a rack of clothes. Alex looks at Samara, scared and weirdly excited. It's obvious no one has ever spoken to the designer like that before. Antonio's face is knotted with rage. He topples a dress form to the ground, and it falls mere inches from hitting her.

"Why did I even bother hiring you if you don't know what I want?" Antonio is radiating fury at her and she doesn't know what to do.

Everything in the room is silent except for Antonio's heavy breathing. Samara stares at the headless mannequin, lifeless on the floor. She feels like the dress form, clueless and unable to move.

"I'll take care of it," she eventually says, and carefully steps over the mannequin. She leaves the room, taking Rosa with her, while the designer screams at her to return.

"What are you going to do?" Rosa asks, on the verge of tears. Samara deposits her at hair and makeup.

"Can you touch her up, please?" Samara sounds like a robot, holding her anxiety in but afraid it will spill out anyway. She walks out the main entrance and stands in front of the building.

"Fuck," she says. "Fuck me."

Antonio is about to fire her ass and send her right back to Jersey. This can't be how she's let go, over some dumb photo shoot. Alex texts her to come back inside. Instead, Samara covers her face with her hands, digging her nails into her scalp until she feels pain.

A young woman walks up to her, coming from the direction of the slaughterhouse. Her determined stride draws Samara's attention. The woman wears a cream button-up shirt with slightly puffed short sleeves and a mid-length flared skirt. Her brown hair is parted to the side and graces her shoulders in loose waves. She has large brown eyes and a sorrowful expression. Samara can't tell what age she is. She could be sixteen or she could be twenty-six.

"Are you here for the photo shoot?" Samara asks, practically running up to her. "Consuelo's?"

The woman nods.

"¡Venga! Come!" Samara can't believe her luck. With her striking looks that seem to come from another time, she would make a perfect Ramona.

Samara gently touches the woman's arm. A sudden chill—un

escalofrío—inches up the back of Samara's neck, but she hurries on.

Inside, Antonio continues to rant. The woman stops before the closed door, afraid to enter.

"He's not going to do anything to you," Samara says. "Se lo prometo. Promise."

She urges her forward.

"What about her?" Samara asks, interrupting the designer mid-tantrum. "Antonio, she's exactly what you're looking for."

He flashes a fake grin and walks up to the woman. Antonio cups her cheeks, examining her strong features. The woman's eyes stay glued on Samara. She's afraid, but Samara ignores it.

"*This* is what I mean," Antonio says. "Where were you hiding her?"

Everyone in the room erupts in laughter, but not the factory worker. Her concerned expression lifts only when Samara leads her away from Antonio.

When the woman steps into The Ramona dress, it fits her perfectly. Her curves are accentuated in the red leather and lace without appearing vulgar. The severe neckline gracefully follows her smooth clavicle better than any dress form.

Samara instructs that her makeup not be too extreme. The woman doesn't need it. Her natural complexion hints at a small amount of color on her lips and cheeks. She appears flushed, like she's been out in the cold.

"You're so beautiful," Samara says. "How do you say 'ravishing' in Spanish?"

"Encantadora," the woman says, admiring her reflection in the full-length mirror.

Antonio's no longer raging. Eventually, he's confident enough with the project to leave and allow everyone to do their jobs. This stranger has saved her.

"¿Cómo se llama?"

When the woman says her name, Samara immediately forgets it.

SAMARA AND ALEX stand over the photographer, editing the pictures. There are so many to choose from. Each image with the factory worker is of her looking straight into the camera, her expression deadly in every shot. She is cold and gorgeous. A Ramona through and through.

Samara's favorite image is that of the woman sitting, her legs slightly crossed, with Rosa standing beside her. The Ramona dress drapes perfectly on her, following the contours of her body and creating a deep contrast from the restrained siren look Rosa employs. Meat hooks dangle above their heads. The two striking women convey equal parts fearlessness and sexuality.

"Where is she?" Samara asks. "Did she leave already?"

No one remembers the woman's name. They try out different ones—Maria, Lupe—racist jokes Samara doesn't call them out on because she's too happy with the results of the shoot.

"Did she speak to you?" Samara asks Rosa.

"No, she just kept whispering," she says. "I think she was humming to herself or praying."

"Praying? She wasn't the only one," Samara says with a nervous grin.

When Antonio calls Samara to his office, she thinks he's going to apologize, maybe even admit she was right all along. What Samara doesn't expect is to see a sour-looking Dolores standing there.

"We're still going through the images," Samara says. "But we should have the edit for you to look at soon."

"No, that's not what I want to talk to you about," he says.

"Did you confer with Dolores about using Rosa in the photo shoot?'

Samara can't believe it.

"I don't understand," she says, trying not to sound angry. "I figured Rosa works for you, Antonio. We are all on the same team, right?"

Dolores stares at Samara like she's a bad girl doing bad things. Antonio gets up and presses Samara's shoulder, consoling her for the apparent mishap. So much drama for no reason.

"Samara, it's important you work with Dolores on anything involving her department. From now on, none of the seamstresses will be used for campaigns. Understood?"

This is such a stupid mandate, but all Samara does is nod. Dolores is angry and trying to rein her in, but it won't work. Antonio is happy with the photo shoot.

"Of course. It will never happen again," she says. "Antonio, let me show you the one picture I love so much!"

She pulls the image already stored on her phone. So what if there's a new mandate in place? The results of Samara's ideas are stunning.

Dolores doesn't bother to stay to see the photo, but Samara is right—Antonio loves the image too.

CHAPTER 16

ALEX AIR-KISSES the owner of the bar and introduces Samara before the group is whisked away to a corner banquette. The Vernon Speakeasy has a very 1900s-inspired interior design, with stamped tin plates covering the ceiling and glass decanters lining the bar. Whiffs of molasses punctuate the air while model-like servers hand out glowing green glasses of absinthe. Located right in the center of the city, the bar is an ideal place for the Antonio Mota crew.

Even after a long day on the shoot, no one says no to drinks after—definitely not Samara, who feels vindicated. Victorious. The photo shoot was a success and she plans to mark her one-month anniversary living in this city by partying with her co-workers.

"Oh shit, this is my jam!" she screams when an old J.Lo song plays. Those seated at the table laugh at her, but Samara still sings "Get Right" and dances with Alex while they're both seated in their chairs.

People swing by their booth—stylists from magazines, starlets hoping for free dresses, publicists trying to get their attention. Samara's group grows more and more obnoxious as the night wears on. Those wanting to talk business are shooed away. Only people who want to get as obliterated as them are allowed in their circle.

"Brandon! Over here!" Tommy yells.

As he walks toward them, Samara does a quick face check. She's buzzed, but not stupid. Her makeup's still flawless. Good.

"Enchantée." Samara holds her hand out for Brandon to kiss. He replies in French. "I don't know what the fuck you're saying but you can keep saying it." Brandon lightly caresses her fingers.

"I said your beautiful hands are cold. Let me warm them." She finds his delivery is not street-smooth like the guys she used to ignore in Jersey. Still, something about his beard and the hints of chest hair peeking out from under his top-unbuttoned shirt does it for her.

"Thanks for the Farmhouse," Samara says. "You saved my ass."

"Of course," he says. "I'm here to serve."

"What other services do you provide?"

"They're exclusive and top-notch. Only the best. Do you want to sample?"

They continue like this. Corny banter that works on her, for the most part. He leans in close. He smells like money and sex.

"Your glass is empty. Let me fix that."

She stares at his backside and imagines what it would be like to fuck him. Would he be rough? Choke her? Would he whisper to her in Spanish? It's been forever since she got laid. The last time was with a friend of the family, a recent transplant from Miami. Every word out of his mouth was a Pitbull quote, and she'd fucked him hard in his rental car just to shut him up.

Tommy pokes her. "You down with that?" he asks.

"What's the bochinche?" Samara asks.

Tommy asks what "bochinche" means and tells everyone at their table, excited for the new vocabulary. "The bochinche is he has big dick energy and can back it up. He only fucks with strong women but is very discreet."

"Would Antonio be upset if he knew I was talking to him?" she asks, impressed by how she can even think of covering her ass before she tries to bring that BDE her way.

"Antonio doesn't care who you fuck unless you're messy at work. Are you messy?"

"Okay, I get it." She takes what Tommy says as a warning. Maybe she should forget how horny she is and stay clear of Brandon.

When Brandon returns to the table to deliver her drink, a man pulls him away before she can thank him. The night progresses and Samara loses sight of him, but at least the drinks don't stop. She can barely stand up. Everyone is drunk, but she feels it more. Tommy's warning echoes in her head.

"Be right back," she says and leaves them for the very small dance floor. She moves to the music for several songs. Strobe lights blink on and off, adding to the frenzy. Brandon grins at her from the edge of the dance floor and she keeps moving her hips, turning in her towering heels. Samara gets lost in the rhythm, closing her eyes and letting the music take hold until the lights abruptly turn on.

"What the hell?" She leans on a server bussing a table near her for support.

"Time to go," the server says, but he sounds like an animal barking. Confused, she backs away from him and joins the exodus spilling through the main door.

The crowd in front of the club are all on their phones, ordering car services or waiting for the valet. The price surge is on and so are the delays.

"Forget this." The Murphy can't be too far. The path Samara takes isn't a straight one. Being this drunk is amateur hour. Samara has always been able to separate her drinking from work, only letting herself get stupid around her friends. She can't allow her co-workers to see her this wasted.

She steadies herself and tries to read a street sign. The lamppost barely illuminates the words, or maybe it's just her inebriated state unable to translate. She stands there squinting and wondering which avenue to take.

Footsteps quickly approach and Samara searches for Abuela Lola's scissors, forgetting she didn't have any room in her micropurse to carry them.

"Hey." Someone touches her elbow and she screams.

"You scared the shit out of me!"

"I didn't mean to scare you," Brandon says, laughing. "I just thought you might need a ride."

"No, I'm good." Samara pulls out her phone and angrily taps at it. As much as she wants to go with Brandon, she knows she shouldn't. He's a red flag. "Thanks, but I'm waiting for a Lyft."

"Have a good night then," he says and heads to his parked car.

Samara can't even manage to open the app. The screen is a blur. She doesn't recognize the street she's on or know which direction to turn in. She shouldn't go with Brandon, shouldn't say yes to a ride back to her place, and yet . . .

He starts his car.

"Fuck it," she says, then yells for him to wait.

Brandon holds open the door to the passenger seat, offering to help her in.

"I live at The Murphy," she says as he climbs into the driver's seat.

"I know it well," Brandon says. "Are you familiar with the history of The Murphy? The Battle of La Mesa was fought where The Murphy was built. A lot of bloodshed."

Samara opens the window and lets the breeze wake her up a bit. "I hope you're not going to give me a history lesson. I can't right now with this podcast episode of *The True Life of Vernon.*"

She's being a bitch, but she's also so drunk and horny.

"Sorry, I'm not here to bore you," he says in a deep voice. "I promise to up my game."

Samara faces him and grins. "You better."

THERE ARE GAPS in her memory. One moment she's in his car and staring at his lips. Another they're both inside the elevator and her body is pressed against his. Tongue in mouth. Nails digging into his back. When they enter her apartment, he takes control and roughly throws her on the bed. The room spins and she likes this feeling of drowning, of going under.

But as the hours pass, she becomes confused by the placement of his hands. There are disturbing animal noises. Something trying to scurry free. The bleeding woman she saw on the street appears and reaches out to Samara.

"Wait," Samara says, but the grunting sounds are louder.

Brandon flips her onto her stomach. The blood-soaked hands recede into a dark corner of the room.

"You're not like the others," a voice says, but it's not Brandon who is speaking. Samara winces when the voice repeats itself.

She loses track of her own body and pleasure, and she's too scared to say anything. Afraid she is overreacting or is wasted. Or, it's her mother's voice telling her "El hombre es prometer y prometer hasta meter, y despues de lo metido, nada de lo prometido." This goes on forever and she can't stop it.

There is a moment when she experiences another shift. This time she views what's happening to her from up on the ceiling, disconnected from her own body. From above she can see how Brandon is now on top of her and how he presses his fingers onto her throat. At first she likes it, but then she can't breathe. Her legs buck underneath him like a horse. Brandon's beady eyes are red and drops of sweat land on her. Somewhere in the room, a person is laughing or crying, but Samara can't be sure if it's her weeping.

When she eventually comes to, her eyes open to his clothes on the floor. His shirt atop her outfit. Someone moves next to her, followed by the sound of footsteps. Samara clutches the sheet for protection. When Brandon returns with a glass, he leans down and kisses her, coating her throat with the coolness of water.

"Am I dreaming?" she asks but no one answers.

Time passes and she once again awakens to the slamming of a door.

It's three in the morning and Samara is alone.

CHAPTER 17

To cut through how fat and heavy her tongue feels, Samara pours a miniature bottle of dark rum into her steaming cup of black coffee. The heat scalds her throat so much that she reaches up to soothe it. The pressure from her hand reminds her of last night and she scrambles to remember more, but the memory is fleeting. This is the first time she's ever blacked out from drinking too much; the first time she's let a drink take her over the edge. Samara's unsure of what happened and this scares her. She doesn't know if Brandon crossed a line. Is she at fault for not being conscious through parts of it?

She feels too stupid to ask anyone, definitely not Brandon. Instead, she sips the scalding coffee, her burnt tongue a punishment. Maybe the pain will jar the memories awake, snap her out of this fog so she can create a timeline and place the pieces together.

Or does it even matter? There was pleasure in there. Hints of it pop up in her mind and she clings to those glimpses like an anchor.

It took everything in her to make it to work, to haul herself away from staring at the crack in the ceiling. When she showered she counted the scratches on her body. Samara did enjoy herself. But what about the other stolen pockets of time? Of the fucked-up visions that joined her in that apartment?

No pasó nada. Nothing happened that she didn't want. She tries to convince herself while swallowing the café fuerte down. This morning drink, she swears, is only a hangover cure—the medicine to help her ease this growing doubt.

Lake softly knocks on Samara's door, holding a large bouquet of flowers. Samara nods at her to enter.

"These came for you," she says. "Do you want me to set them on your desk?"

She hands Samara the note attached to the gaudy arrangement. Samara tries to hide behind the mug.

"Are you okay?" Lake asks. "I saw you briefly last night but then you disappeared. Did you have fun?"

Technically Lake's job title is receptionist. She's the first person visitors encounter when entering the building. But like everyone who works for Antonio, her duties also include being one of his assistants. Lake is privy to all the gossip. She knows who is on the outs with Antonio way before the victim is aware. That she had eyes on Samara makes her nervous. How bad did she look last night?

"I did have fun," she says, trying to sound natural. "Did you?"

"Oh yeah. The music was so good," Lake says. She lingers in the office, fiddling with the floral display. "I noticed you were talking to Brandon."

Lake's mentioning her interaction with Brandon means

others noticed it, too, and that's not a good thing. Tommy told her not to be messy, and she fucked up, didn't take heed of his warning. Samara treads cautiously.

"I was thanking him for helping with the photo shoot," Samara says, cupping the mug with both hands to help stop the tremors.

"Everyone knows Brandon," Lake says, grinning conspiratorially. "I owe him so much. If it wasn't for him, I would still be working at the factory."

"The factory?"

"Consuelo's, of course." Lake sweeps off fallen petals from the desk and drops them into the garbage can. "Antonio needed a front person. Brandon saw me working on the slaughterhouse floor and he just knew I would be perfect. He's always looking out for us."

"Us?" Samara asks.

"Yes, us. Latinas. He wants the best for us. He's a good person to have on your side."

Lake glances at the sealed card then back to Samara.

"I'd better get back to my desk. Let me know if you want to take something to help with that hangover."

"I don't have a hangover," Samara says with a straight face and waits for Lake to leave before opening the envelope.

Thinking of you and last night—B

Across the way, Dolores gets up from her workstation. She glances over to the flowers and adjusts her sweater. Does she know about Brandon as well? Does everyone? Samara gives Dolores her back and sneaks another splash of rum into her mug.

She's crossing another disturbing line. Like the blackout, this is also the first time she's ever drank so early in the morning, not counting mimosas during brunch dates. But this is different. It's hard not to mark this moment, how the shakes can't possibly be just from today's hangover. She places the empty bottle in the trash and covers it with Brandon's note.

"Where did you run off to, Samara?" Tommy hollers from across the workroom. To stop him from airing out her business, Samara walks over to him with a quick clip.

"Please shut up," she says.

"You're not the only one." He gestures around. Their coworkers clutch their cups of coffee like a life raft, unlike Tommy, who is alert and fresh.

"How are you even walking?" Samara asks.

"Last night was nothing to my usual." He leans on a mannequin. "So, give me the rundown. What happened?"

"Nothing. I went home and slept it off," Samara says. This is work and no one will find out about her night, especially not when she's still trying to figure it out.

"Someone said they saw you get into Brandon's car," he says. "Or was that just a hallucination they had?"

"That must have been some other Latina," Samara says. Tommy's grin is bright, but she doesn't break.

"Are you talking about last night? I don't remember a thing." Alex joins them. She, too, doesn't look half as bad as Samara. "Someone here still smells like alcohol."

Samara takes a step back. Tommy finds a sample of Antonio's perfume and spritzes the air with it. The tips of Samara's fingers vibrate.

"Those drinks were so potent," Alex says. "I'm never drinking again."

"You mean you're never drinking again *today*," Tommy says. "Talk to me tomorrow and we'll see how you feel."

It hurts to laugh, but Samara still joins in. She wants to ask them all types of questions, like how was she last night and was she really that bad off, but to do so would be to admit she has no clue how drunk she was. The others continue to go over the events. They ended up at some after-hours in a downtown loft. The festivities didn't stop until three in the morning when they finally ordered car services to take them home safely.

"Where did you disappear to?" Alex asks.

"I was looking for you but when I went back to the table, you were all gone," she says. "I got a ride home. I'm from Jersey, I can take care of myself."

They start to crack jokes about Jersey, interspersing New York badass girls with clichéd Jersey tropes. Big hair, bigger knives.

"There was a moment when I swore I was levitating, that's how fucked up I was," Alex says.

The seamstresses look up and shake their heads at the group. Dolores holds Samara's stare. The weight of Samara's tongue continues to bother her, but at least she's calibrated her alcohol intake just enough to beat the hangover. She can control *something* about her body. The other things—the question marks about last night—bear so heavily on her that she forms the next question delicately.

"It was fun, wasn't it?" Her question is more a plea than anything. She needs confirmation that it *was* fun, to help dissolve the pit inside of her.

"It was! It was so much fun!"

Everyone chimes in at the same time, a chorus of validation. When she hears the words, she feels a sense of relief. Maybe it *was* all okay. So what if she can't remember? Others remember the night, and that makes it seem fine.

She spends the rest of the morning in her office, convincing herself that she's safe. She texts her Jersey group chat and they celebrate her first West Coast dick. It *is* a celebration. For once,

Samara is the one with a salacious story to tell them and not the other way around. She takes a picture of the floral arrangement and sends it to them.

We're so proud of you, Angie writes. *Now don't ever speak about or talk to him again. He was just practice.*

The more her friends tell her she's leveled up, the quicker her confusion diminishes. She moves the flowers from her desk where Lake placed them. She doesn't want to have them in her view, to be a reminder of that night. Instead, she relocates them to a far corner of the room, out of her line of sight.

All day, Samara constructs a neatly tied narrative compiled by her co-workers where the night was nothing but diversion, nothing but a delight, a strange, wild memory. There's a false sense of freedom when she lets go of her doubts. It's especially easy after she finds an unopened bottle of a new coffee liqueur that was gifted to her a couple of weeks ago. The drink is too sweet, a poor imitation of Bailey's, but it helps.

CHAPTER 18

JANUARY 10

ONE MONTH UNTIL THE FASHION SHOW

ALTHOUGH THE MODEL is barefoot, her gait is so loud that Samara's mug vibrates. To avoid any accidental spillage, Samara lifts the cup and drinks. The vodka coats her belly nicely. Ever since the night with Brandon, she's taken to adding a splash or two of alcohol to her morning coffee. Just a little. Samara swears she read somewhere how vodka with coffee is practically a healthy, odorless tonic. Her morning drink is just like taking a vitamin; it leaves her feeling even-keeled and keeps her thoughts from racing too far into the past. It's simpler to live in a murky haze—to live in the gray—and not question anything too deeply.

"The neckline should not fall that way," Antonio says. Tommy pins the fabric to the designer's specifications.

Antonio has multiple iPads open in front of him. While the model changes, his assistants show him accessories in need of approval. Samara's latest draft of the one-pager lies in front of Antonio with a slash across the whole thing. Dead on arrival.

"Samara, do you understand what I'm looking for?" Antonio

asks with impatience. He's been ranting for the past ten minutes about what's wrong with the draft she submitted to him. "If your writing doesn't highlight the essence of what I'm saying with my collection, then there's no point to it. I can't keep repeating myself."

She nods and writes the word "essence" in her notebook before circling it.

Samara's gold star has been slowly dimming. The glow from the photo shoot lasted a good week and change, and Samara rode that aura of brilliance hard. But when she delivered her one-pager describing Antonio's upcoming collection, her beautiful fall began. Antonio hates every single draft she's shown him. He says her work lacks any depth, that she's missing the point.

She wonders if this has anything to do with her night with Brandon. Did he find out? Samara hasn't spoken to Brandon, not even to thank him for the flowers. No one at work has mentioned him at all, and even if they did think she fucked him, she would deny that shit to the grave. Tommy warned her Antonio does not tolerate disorder, and she's really trying to keep it together, minus the vodka in coffee. *Ignore the vodka,* she tells herself.

"I understand," she says, but she really doesn't. The more iterations she creates, the more annoyed Antonio becomes. He hasn't thrown anything, like the time at the photo shoot, but it's in the air, the threat of it. Like a child in time-out, Samara stares at the design the model's wearing and waits for Antonio to dismiss her so she can return to her office to find the "essence" of the clothes.

"Let's see look number eight again," Antonio says.

This isn't exactly what Samara imagined life would be like

working for him. She'd pictured herself acting more like a muse, guiding a great artist out of a brand's complacency, helping him decide what works or doesn't work. Instead, Samara searches for clues while jotting down notes to save her life.

The bored model reenters the room wearing a black suit with crimson fringe dragging on the floor from each cuff. The way the fringe spills to the ground reminds Samara of the woman with the bleeding hands. To erase the memory, she guzzles down her spiked coffee, letting the burn snap her out of it.

"No, the sleeves aren't right," Antonio says. "Do them over."

At least Samara isn't the only star that's falling. The designs Tommy and the rest of the team have been creating are sexy and bold, but sometimes they venture too far from Antonio's preferred silhouette. When that happens, the designer harshly pulls them back. As the fashion show draws nearer, no one is above getting knocked down a peg by the boss. With the two runway shows happening on both coasts, the designers must finish early to get Antonio's approval before he flies to New York to concentrate on that show.

"This is how I want the pants to fall," he says firmly. "You and Samara need to pay attention to the tiny details instead of having me point it out. It's why I hired you."

He gets up and roughly plays with the garment. The model is unfazed. She stands perfectly still, but deep inside Samara wishes the model would plunge a high heel into Antonio's chest.

"Sorry to bother you, Antonio." Lake enters the room. "Olivia is still expecting you today. Should I reschedule?"

"Yes, reschedule. I'm too busy right now. She'll understand."

Antonio goes back to the suit, but before Lake leaves, he changes his mind. "This might be good for Samara. Send her instead."

"Okay, I'll let Olivia and Dolores know," Lake says and leaves.

"Sure, I'll go," Samara says with enthusiasm. She'll do anything to avoid staring at the blank screen until tears form in her eyes. "Who is Olivia?"

"If you don't know who Olivia Celis is, we've got bigger problems than your writing," he says.

He's being such a bitch, but Samara asks him anyway, "Celis, as in the same family who owned the Celis Knitting Mills?"

"Yes. There would be no Vernon if it weren't for the Celis family," Antonio says while directing the designers to create darts along the pant leg.

Abuela Lola had recounted countless stories of her time as a Celis Knitting Mills employee. All those long hours she labored in that factory, working on so many designs, clothing Hollywood movie stars. She never once received any recognition for her work, and so Samara made sure to write about that exploitation in her personal essay. What would Abuela Lola want her to say to Olivia?

"What's the occasion for the visit?" Samara asks while she gathers her things.

"A fitting," he says. "Just go and send Olivia my love."

Samara walks to Seamstress Row in search of the doña to find only Dolores's sweater draped over the back of the chair.

"She's waiting for you in the parking lot," Rosa says.

Ever since the photo shoot, Rosa has slowly shed her conservative church attire, showing a bit more skin each day. Today she's in a short floral shirt dress, the cross that was once around her neck nowhere to be found. Samara takes credit for this rebellious change in Rosa. Samara and the rest of the wild ones are rubbing off on her, and that must annoy Dolores.

"I wish I was going with you," Rosa says. "I'm so tired of looking at this zipper."

"Do you want to trade places?" Samara asks. "I'll deal with the zipper and you can spend your day with Dolores."

Rosa laughs. "No, I think I'd better stay."

Although it's been a couple of weeks since the photo shoot, Dolores still displays a cold front to Samara, only giving one-word answers whenever Samara asks her a question. The harder Dolores tries to keep tight her circle of seamstresses, the more Samara wants to penetrate it, but she will do so with kindness. She'll meet Dolores's icy exterior with sweetness, even if it's fake.

Samara heads toward the parking lot but Rosa stops her.

"I was meaning to ask you something." She tucks a loose strand of hair behind her ear. "I don't know if you're looking for an assistant, but maybe I can help. You always seem so busy."

"Oh. I'm sorry. I have an assistant already." Samara feels bad for Rosa. She's so eager to lend a hand no matter the department. For Rosa, there is no work hierarchy. "You don't like working with Dolores?"

"I love Dolores, but she's like my mother. So strict," she says. "They treat me like I'm their baby, the seamstresses."

"Don't worry, I'll ask around," Samara says. "I'm sure there must be someone who can use you."

She feels an affinity for Rosa, can relate to what she's going through since it was only a few weeks ago that she was in a similar position with her family. There's nothing wrong with trying to assert a bit of independence, to forge a path of your own.

"Thank you so much!" Rosa hugs her tight and Samara laughs.

"But I haven't done anything yet!"

"You're the only person who cares what happens to me." Rosa's voice quivers, unable to hold back her emotions. This breaks Samara's heart.

"I promise to help," she says.

CHAPTER 19

Dolores has the radio tuned to Christian music. The music isn't loud but it's more than enough to make Samara want to jump out of the moving car. The doña softly hums along to the song about heaven and God and sacrifice.

"Is the church you attend the one located near The Murphy on Soto?" Samara asks. "I walk past it all the time. It seems really old."

"I attend every morning," she says. "All of my girls do."

"Do they have to attend church to be able to work with you?" It's an obnoxious thing to ask, but Samara can't stop her mouth from moving. Maybe it's the music that's getting to her, or maybe it's just how Dolores's dour expression is always so hard to penetrate.

"Everyone can benefit from it," Dolores says. "Even you."

"If I enter a church I'll probably go up in flames," Samara says, but what she really thinks is how churches remind her of death and sinful acts she would much rather forget. Dolores doesn't say anything. They drive in silence.

The Celis estate is hidden behind imposing black gates and dense hedges. The gate automatically opens and Dolores drives to the back of the house. She carries her sewing kit with her, her face a mask of deep concentration. The seamstress never seems to relax. Even when Dolores was singing softly to the church music, her actions felt like she was proving to her God that even when she's riding along with a sinner, she's always doing right by Him.

Before Dolores rings the bell they're met by a Latina in a traditional black-and-white maid's uniform with a full apron. It's shocking to see how antiquated and ridiculous her appearance is. The woman nods slightly and lets them in.

"I'm upstairs, Dolores. Come." An elderly voice wafts down and the servant gestures for them to follow it.

The Celis home is filled with pricey antiques, fireplaces, and original paintings of important—and most likely dead—white men. Samara feels like she's entered a restored historical house that has been converted into a museum. There's even an old Victrola. As Samara trails behind Dolores up the grand staircase, she takes in the framed newspaper clippings on the walls detailing the history of Vernon, with its lush gardens and beautiful parks to linger in. "An idyllic place to live!" shout the headlines.

Seated in a French tufted chair like a queen is Olivia Celis in head-to-toe Chanel. The logo-heavy outfit hangs off of her shrinking frame. The clothes seem to have been selected because of the label and not for how they will enhance her figure. Every single finger has a large stone ring: diamonds, sapphires, garnets. Even her wrists are covered with gold bangles. She's giving Iris Apfel, minus the big glasses.

"Hello, my name is Samara Martín. Antonio sends his regrets," she says. "He was called away on an emergency, but I'm here to help."

"Samara? Is that Indian?"

Samara could tell this was going to be a long meeting with a geriatric racist, but this is nothing new to her. She's been in this exact same predicament before, at galas surrounded by rich people who invited her because they're craving a little flavor and spend the whole time trying to figure out "where she's *really* from" over hors d'oeuvres.

"No, I'm Cuban, from New York," she says. "I started with Antonio a month ago."

"How is it that the workers he hires keep getting younger, Dolores, while we continue to age?" Olivia grabs Samara's hand and leads her to the sofa. Dolores places a wooden stepstool in front of a gold, ornate, full-length mirror.

"Do you like your job? What do you do besides having to entertain this old lady?"

Samara gives her the abbreviated history, making sure to amp up her career highlights. If Olivia is important to Antonio, she wants to make sure the woman likes her.

"He's so brilliant at what he does," Samara says. "I'm so lucky to get to learn from him."

The uniformed maid from earlier walks in with a tray of tea and crackers.

"You two could almost be sisters," Olivia says.

There's absolutely no resemblance between Samara and the maid, only skin tone, but Samara is all grins at Olivia. The maid silently walks across the plush, carpeted floor, never lifting her head once.

Dolores hangs four different gowns on a wardrobe stand for Olivia to try on. She takes out her pincushion and hangs her measuring tape around her neck.

"Is this for a special occasion?" Samara asks and helps the woman to her feet so she can undress in a curtained section of the room.

"These are going to be for the dinner I'm hosting for Antonio. You'll be there, won't you?"

This is the first time Samara is hearing about the event and she's worried that this lack of information may not be a mistake. Is she being iced out already? She prays that's not the case.

"Of course. I'll be there," she says.

Dolores helps the woman undress while Samara takes a moment to look at the many framed pictures on a circular table. The photographs depict a timeline that starts somewhere in the 1900s and ends sometime in the seventies. Each decade highlights a different California fashion era. However, the one constant in these pictures is the uniformed help, dressed in the same outfit as Olivia's current maid, and holding trays of food or standing poised with arms pressed firmly to their sides.

"What you're looking at is Vernon history," Olivia says. "My family were early inhabitants. We've seen the changes firsthand and weathered many storms. We've always had high hopes for Vernon. We knew that eventually everyone would come to see this place as the jewel it really is."

Samara lifts up a black-and-white photo of two women. One is wearing a cinched blazer over a full skirt popularized back in the 1940s, while the other woman stands behind her, head down, wearing a maid's uniform. "Is this you?"

"Yes, it is! I was quite the looker back then." Dolores zips up a fitted black silhouette with tiny gold buttons that follow Olivia's spine like a snake.

"And the woman standing behind you?"

"No one," she says.

It's amazing to think photographic evidence of a human can mean nothing to a person. What's so striking is how identical the photo looks to the campaign Samara just finished wrapping up. History repeating itself—but this time, with Samara recreating it for money.

Another framed photo taken from an even earlier period of time. A portrait of a woman definitely kin to Olivia. They have the same pointy chin and bob-length hairstyle. The regally dressed woman stands in front of a building and is surrounded by men in tailored suits. Beneath the photo is a typewritten caption announcing the grand opening of the Celis Knitting Mills.

"Who is this in front of the Knitting Mills?" Samara asks. "She looks so much like you."

"That is my great-great-grandmother," she says. Dolores goes down on her knees to pin the length of the gown.

"I had family that worked at the Mills," Samara says. "She was a talented seamstress. You've probably heard of her. Her name was Dolores Sanz."

"Oh that's nice," the old woman says, and Samara can't tell if she's referring to the gown or to what Samara just said. She wants to shake the woman until her jewelry falls off and she acknowledges her grandmother, but Abuela Lola was just one of hundreds of workers who passed through the factory. When Samara wrote her piece, she had read how they shut their doors a couple of years ago, a casualty of the COVID-19 pandemic.

"What happened to the Knitting Mills?" she asks.

"Closed, even after all we did for the community. They accused my family of poisoning people," Olivia says. "Remember, Dolores? How they came after my name, forgetting the vast sums of money we've donated to help rebuild this city. The jobs we created. They threw it all in our faces."

Olivia gets more and more agitated. Samara ignores the cues to stop asking questions. She's so fascinated by the photos and the way every single white person is being served by someone brown.

"That doesn't make any sense. What were the accusations tied to?" Samara asks, not really thinking through how her intrusive questions might land.

Olivia abruptly climbs down from the stepstool. She grabs the frame from Samara and places it loudly back on the table.

"Lies. Such horrible, dirty people. Liars, all of them."

The anger in the woman's eyes startles Samara because it feels familiar, this flash of rage.

"I'm sorry," Samara says. The room suddenly feels so stuffy. She pulls at her collar and fans herself with her hand. It's so hot. If she stays in the room she'll faint. She needs to get out of there.

"I have a call to make. Is it okay if I step out for a second?"

"Yes, go," Dolores says. The seamstress has been quiet the whole time until now, her stern expression revealing her disappointment.

Samara walks out to the hallway and wipes the sweat above her lip. A French window is ajar and she plants herself in front of it to try to cool down.

Dirty people. Liars.

The maid walks toward her, her eyes downcast. Her steps are so strong and determined. Even with her head down, Samara can see the woman is also angry. Was she in the room during Olivia's outburst? Yes, Samara remembers her clearing the table. The woman holds the silver tray with the uneaten crackers still on it. Samara offers a weak smile as she draws nearer.

"Cochinos."

"Excuse me," Samara says, unsure of what she heard. "What did you say?"

But the maid soundlessly walks away, leaving Samara doubting she heard anything at all.

CHAPTER 20

THE NEXT DAY, Samara doesn't mention to Antonio how distraught the old woman became during the fitting.

"Olivia was so happy! She can't wait to celebrate you," she says instead in her most extreme white girl voice to the designer, who's sitting with his back to her. "Is there anything you need me to do for the dinner she's hosting?"

"What dinner?" he asks, engrossed in his mood board.

Samara acts like he's joking and laughs, a big goofy cackle that sounds unnatural. When he doesn't join in, she tries to play it off, but it's too late. The lack of an invite means she's still on the outs.

"Olivia mentioned the dinner she's planning for you, which is so sweet of her," she babbles on. "She was so lovely. It's such a shame what happened to the Knitting Mills."

"Do you have something for me?" Antonio cuts her off. "Instead of worrying about a dinner, you should be working."

He's very calm, and that feels even more disconcerting. She's fucking up. The one-pager still hasn't met his approval and she's past due on submitting another draft. There's no excuse.

"I'm almost done. I'll have it to you by the end of the day," she says. Samara hasn't written a thing. "Let me get back to it."

She spends all day staring at her screen, clutching her mug filled half with coffee and half with vodka and freaking out over the lack of a dinner invite.

Last night, Samara dreamt about Olivia. In her dream the old woman stood in front of a wooden pulpit, reciting the words *dirty people* over and over again in a trance. Olivia then slowly fed gleaming, silver pins into her maid's mouth while Samara screamed at her to stop.

She woke up in a cold sweat to strange grunting sounds again. It was two in the morning, because lately it seems like it's always two in the morning in her apartment. And like every night since she moved in, Samara stared at the crack in the ceiling, waiting for something to happen, for the noise to stop or get louder. For a voice to speak to her. Anything. The volume increased alongside Samara's anxiousness until she got up from her bed and drank half a bottle of wine.

Still, she managed to make it to work on time, ready to write, only to be consumed by her last interaction with Antonio. As the day drags on, no one bothers her because they don't want to catch the failure virus she's emitting. Besides, she's so busy typing up words and deleting them, typing and deleting. Samara stays glued to her seat, praying the elixir she drinks—her vodka and coffee—will jolt her out of this stupid writing slump.

Procrastinating under the guise of research, she types the name "Olivia Celis" and "the Celis Knitting Mills" into the search bar. There are many articles highlighting the charitable donations and grand openings the family has been connected to over the years, documentation of all the good they've done for Vernon, with Olivia always in the center of it. But buried deep in the search results is an article—the one Samara's been looking for. The article says that Celis Knitting Mills had been accused of environmental crimes, of poisoning the Vernon community. Hundreds of factory workers and families fell sick with strange ailments and cancers. Some even died.

"No wonder Olivia was so mad," Samara says.

A class action lawsuit was filed against the family, accusing them of covering up the leaks and avoiding the necessary cleanup. Soon after, the factory closed down without much fanfare.

"Are you almost done?" Alex asks before heading to the parking lot. The Saprophyte has emptied out; even Antonio left hours ago.

Samara quits the article from her computer screen before Alex notices what she's reading.

"Almost done!" Samara says with glee, sounding like a demented game show contestant.

"Didn't you just fall in love with Olivia?" Alex asks. "She's such a character."

"Oh my god, I did. She's so great. So what's up with that dinner? When I met with Antonio this morning he didn't mention it at all."

"Ugh. I've been in so many meetings about it," Alex says. "Antonio is driving me crazy."

"Oh yeah, I bet," Samara says. "If you need any help, I'd be more than happy to lend a hand."

"No, we've got it," Alex says. "Well, I'll see you tomorrow."

Samara tries not to be upset. It's all a conspiracy to keep her from being Antonio's favorite again. She just has to get her shit together.

When everyone's gone, Samara walks to the cafeteria in search of something to eat. She's not drunk, but she's almost there. Food will help. The box of Real World Donuts she finds is not exactly what she had in mind, but it'll do. As she eats, her eyes wander to the photos of old Vernon and land on one particular image of a simple wooden building with a large sign atop it reading "The Tailor." Two white men stand in front of the structure. In the image, the curtain from the shop is pulled back, and peeking out from behind is the face of another woman. Samara hasn't noticed this before. She steps closer to get a better view.

The hair on the back of Samara's neck stands on end and she feels her face heating up in a sudden flush of fever. Samara knows this woman's face. She's seen it before.

"It can't be," she says.

The woman looks exactly like the person they photographed for the campaign. *Exactly* like her, with the same dark expression.

"That's . . . that's crazy." Samara presses so close to the photograph that her breath condenses on the surface of the glass. "What was her name?"

She recites different names aloud, trying them on for size, but none rings true until the answer finally clicks.

"Piedad."

The name pops into her head like a thunderclap. Samara is transported to the day she saw that name sewn into Antonio's archives. It makes no sense. How can the woman who came to her to model for an ad look so much like the woman in this old photograph? It could be the woman's kin, but no. Her features are identical. There's no question. This is the woman who posed for them.

"Piedad," she repeats.

The automatic lights in the cafeteria suddenly turn off, and she gasps. They're meant to do that if there's no movement after a set period of time, but it still puts her on edge. She's alone in the building. It's late and dark out.

"I need to get out of here," Samara says, embarrassed by how jumpy she is. The lights fail to turn back on, so she walks fast to her office. She quickly gathers her things and grabs Abuela Lola's scissors, shoving them in her purse like she always does. Samara walks past Seamstress Row and heads toward the parking lot. But when she reaches the Library, she stops.

Someone or something pounds on the red door.

"Hello! Is there someone there? Tommy?"

She calls the names of other co-workers, but they've left hours ago. She's completely alone. Samara steps closer. The pounding becomes more urgent.

"Go, bitch," she whispers. "Go."

Why can't she run? Why can't she get the fuck out of there? Her legs refuse to obey, curiosity desperate to take the lead.

Then a woman's voice emerges from behind the closed door and begins to sing.

"La zorrita, zorrita, señores, se fue a la loma . . ."

The archives' closet door rattles. The pounding becomes more violent, desperate. All the while, the woman croons.

"Y que sube que baja la torre, diciendo que trae un dolor en el alma . . ."

Samara's whole body trembles as she watches the doorknob slowly turn, her heart in her throat.

CHAPTER 21

"GET AWAY FROM ME!"

Samara runs toward the exit and cuts through the parking lot. The woman's haunting voice pursues her. Cars honk at Samara to get out of the way but she doesn't stop, she keeps moving. Even in her stupid pointy heels, she takes off until she's far enough away, until the singing no longer trails behind her.

She stops in front of a boarded-up body shop. In her hand she clutches Abuela Lola's scissors like a weapon, but she can't even remember when she took them out of her purse. Looking down at them, she breaks down and cries.

Is this job trying to kill her? What is going on? The noises and the strange things that are happening. It's all too much. She can't stop crying.

She doesn't know who to turn to. Abuela Lola was the one person who would know what to do, would explain these things to her. Every morning, her grandmother would ask her about her dreams, then decipher the symbols behind them. If a relative came to her in the form of a bird or if Samara felt herself falling down a black hole, Abuela Lola would explain whether it was anxiety manifesting in her subconscious or just a family friend wanting to bless her. Samara would be content with her translations, but these things she's encountering in Vernon, these *occurrences,* make no sense.

They're not a message. They feel like a curse.

The tears don't stop even when Samara takes deep breaths. She needs to calm down. Desperate, she takes her phone out and makes a call.

"Samara, ¿qué pasó?" Her mother answers, her voice groggy with sleep.

"Mom, I don't know what's happening," Samara says. "I think I'm losing it."

"Ay Dios mío," her mother says. "Just come home. It's okay for you to leave. You can get a job anywhere. Your room is ready. Samara, let me buy you a ticket home."

She tries to compose herself but the more her mother talks, the more she feels parts of her are coming undone.

"I can't take this anymore. Something's not right. I don't know what's going on," she says, the words spilling forth. "I keep hearing things. Seeing things that make no sense. I'm scared."

Samara hears a light switch flick on. Her father no longer snores beside her mother. In the background he asks questions and Samara can imagine how this scene is playing out for her parents. Her mother is probably grabbing a robe while her father turns on all the lights, ready to leap into action.

"What do you mean she's seeing things?" her father asks.

"Cállate. Let her speak."

Her parents argue and regret slowly seeps into Samara's body. She shouldn't have called them. What could they do from Jersey? This was a mistake.

"What is happening, Samara?"

She pauses, unsure what she can say to her parents that would make sense. Her mother is a believer too, but unlike Abuela Lola, her dream interpretations always fell flat. She would find ways to blame the receiver for what was happening in their dreams, the ghostly visits somehow always an indication that they were not living their life correctly.

"It's okay, Samara. It's okay. Come home. That job isn't for you. You weren't ready."

Like a predictable script, the call is being turned into an examination of her faults and weaknesses. The only solution was to stay in Jersey and wallow away her days in grief.

A couple holding hands turns the corner and walks toward Samara. The young pair shares a bottle of beer. Samara composes herself by quickly wiping her tears. On the phone, her mother keeps talking but Samara tunes her out, waiting for the couple to pass.

The girl takes a sip from the beer and offers it to her companion, who does the same. All Samara sees is the drink. It glows in the dark like a beacon of light. Salvation. She nods at them and is even able to pull off a slight grin. The two walk to their car.

"It's the stress," her mother says when Samara falls back into the conversation. "Abuela Lola died and then the thing that happened with your cousin . . ."

Samara shuts down and retreats within herself. She's no longer conversing with her mother. She's outside of her body.

"Samara? Are you listening?"

This is happening to someone else, to another Samara.

"What thing that happened?" she finally says. "Nothing happened. Nothing."

Samara doesn't hear her mother rattle off the reasons why she should have never left Jersey. She's not there. Samara only sees her future and what it will look like if she returns. How she'll never leave that place. How the past will devour her.

"I'm sorry, Mami. I made a mistake," she says, carefully. "It's my fault. I've been watching too many scary movies. I'm sorry I called so late."

"Scary movies? Hija, what's going on over there? You're making me very nervous."

Samara needs to end this call and make sure her family believes she's safe—because she is. Because *this*, whatever this is, it's not going to take away her opportunities, her new life. Samara's worked too hard to get to where she is.

"Lo siento. I didn't mean to wake you." She tries to laugh it off, but sounds hysterical instead. "Everything's fine."

"Samara!"

"I'm going to get off the phone now. I'll call you tomorrow. I promise. Okay?"

She hangs up on her mother's urgent exclamations. Her phone continues to ring but Samara sends the calls to voicemail. She checks her reflection in a store window and cleans away any signs of distress. Nothing will stop her from thriving. Not her parents, not the stress from this job. Returning to Jersey is not an option. She has to make this move work, no matter the cost.

Samara retraces the couple's footsteps. Around the corner, there's a food truck and a handful of people lingering in front of it. She has stumbled upon the tail end of an event at Marisa's gallery. Samara hasn't returned since she purchased that painting for Antonio. She notices a table filled with bottles.

Inside, people look at the paintings of dismembered women while Samara heads straight to the man serving drinks. The shakes subside when she tips back the bottle to her lips.

"I know you," someone says. "You're the one working for that designer."

Marisa faces her.

"Oh, hi. Yes, I'm Samara." It's easy to fall right back into this fake veneer, especially when the alcohol warms her empty stomach. The quicker she drinks, the easier she can forget. "I was just heading home and saw you were open. Sorry if it's a private party. I needed a little something to help me get to my destination."

"Everyone who is a friend of Vernon is welcome. Are you a friend?"

"Yes, I'm a friend," Samara says, holding in a sob caught in her throat. "I am."

"Drink up," Marisa says and clinks her bottle to Samara's. "We're celebrating."

"What are we celebrating?"

"Vernon. Everyone I paint is from this beautiful city. We are more Vernon than Vernon. I'm celebrating us."

Marisa leaves Samara to hug a person holding a piece of art, and Samara walks past a half-eaten cake with the name Marisa written on it. The walls of the gallery are crammed with even more paintings than before of women in everyday poses—every inch of wall covered with floating bodies. Someone dancing with her hip erased. A girl braiding another girl's hair, but with her fingers gone. An elderly lady covered in wrinkles missing her eyes. The paintings are even more disturbing to her now. There's nothing cute or campy about the work. They're gruesome and upsetting.

Samara asks for another drink. Another one to fully erase

the incident at work. Just a few more to bring back the familiar buzz.

"I read about your boss's fashion show. My invite must be missing in the mail," Marisa says, her tone biting. "Can't have a fashion show about Vernon without inviting the people who actually live here."

The artist's stare is so intense. Samara concentrates on the paintings to avoid it.

"Why do you draw women like this, with missing body parts?" she asks.

"It's how I feel," Marisa says. "Not all the time, but sometimes. Don't you feel this way too, like people aren't seeing you fully?"

Samara's eyes well up.

"Thank you so much for the beer," she says before a tear rolls down her cheek. She edges to the door, ready to make her exit. "And congratulations."

"Come by anytime," she says. "We'll talk some more about my city—and bodies."

Samara hurries out. It doesn't take long to find her way home, and when she does, she continues to drink until time blurs.

CHAPTER 22

THE NEXT MORNING, Samara tries to enter the conference room quietly, but as soon as she opens the door everyone turns to her, including Antonio.

"You're late."

"I'm so sorry," she says. Sunglasses cover her bloodshot eyes. Mint candy hopefully camouflages her breath, which reeks of alcohol—though she still remembered to spike her coffee tumbler before getting here. When her alarm went off this morning, she was in the middle of throwing up. The hangover is severe, and she wanted to call in sick but knew she couldn't, especially after receiving an email from Lake reminding her of this morning's meeting. On the short drive in she worked on her laptop, typing as fast as she could while begging the driver to slow down.

"We were just asking about your copy," Antonio says. "I haven't seen anything."

Her stomach churns violently, but there's no food in there,

so the odds of her vomiting in front of everyone are slim. Which is too bad—getting sick would be a welcome distraction.

"I have it right here," she says, clutching her laptop to her chest. Her voice sounds gravelly and raw. The clothes she's wearing are wrinkled and not put together. Even with the makeup Samara forced herself to apply, she looks and feels green. She needs to sleep this state off forever.

"Is this some kind of joke?" Antonio asks.

Alex and Tommy glance at each other. They're seated by Antonio, claiming their rightful positions as the current favorites. No one can or will help Samara climb out of this ditch.

"I'm almost done. I stayed here late last night working on it. It's why I overslept and missed my alarm. I just need to look it over one more time." Her voice seems to lose volume with each sentence.

The reality is Samara isn't sure what shape the copy is in. Last night feels like an eternity ago. Her parents are still trying to reach her. Even now she can feel the phone vibrating, along with her nerves.

"Let me make some printouts." When she leaves the room, she can hear Antonio's curses. The palms of her hands are sweaty.

Another reason for her delay getting to work: Samara was afraid of returning. The red door of the Library looms like a giant heart, but the seamstresses are doing what they always do. There's no singing, only the machines humming. No banging on the door. No evidence of last night's aberration.

Still, her eyes keep looking over to the Library when she should be concentrating on her computer screen and checking her work. Samara searches for the latest draft file, but there are so many. Files with different confusing names in total disarray. She selects a version and skims the contents quickly, typing away without paying attention to mistakes or sentence construction. She sends it to the printer, making enough copies for everyone, and runs back to the conference room. The sunglasses sit atop her head, holding back her stringy hair.

"I've been doing all this research. It's really interesting. I think you're going to love it." Samara is talking so fast her tongue clicks against the roof of her mouth. She sounds manic, but she can't stop herself. "I keep thinking of your clothes and the history of this city and its women, like Piedad—no, I mean—like Ramona. It starts with the Celis family, how they kept constructing these factories and how so many workers died from unknown sicknesses, but Vernon keeps surviving, thriving."

As she goes on with her long-winded explanation, Samara does her best to avoid looking at the bored faces of her coworkers.

"Your designs are invoking a type of uniform," she continues. "Like the ones worn by the workers at the factories. A costume they wore while they were dying. A uniform for the end of life."

Antonio's eyes deaden. They glaze over but she keeps talking. If she stops for even a moment, then she has to think about other things—like how her own world is splintering around her.

"I don't understand what any of this has to do with the collection," Antonio finally says. "Alex, what is she talking about?"

Alex nods her head like she's been engaging with this presentation from the very beginning.

"I think maybe Samara has been digging too deeply. We just need to reel it in a bit," she says. "There's some good stuff in here."

"This isn't the final draft, of course." Samara snatches the paper from Alex and leans into Antonio so he can look at her, validate that she really is in the room, that her words make some kind of sense. "This is what you're striving for—to celebrate your Vernon roots. What happened to those people in those factories is part of the history of this city and part of what inspires you."

Antonio slams the table. "I'm not going to present my clothes while talking about a factory poisoning! Are you mad?"

He pushes the paper away. "I don't want to talk about this anymore."

"Oh," Samara says. Her body folds inward.

"Nothing in this draft talks about my designs. Nothing in here mentions The Ramona. Nothing," he says. "Such a waste of everyone's time. What have you been doing?"

"I, um . . ."

"Alex, take care of this."

Alex takes the paper and runs a pen across it. Then hands it back to Samara.

The damage is done. Antonio is over her and so is everyone else. The meeting ends with him storming out.

"What the fuck, Samara?" Tommy asks. "You're really on something. Did you forget who you work for?"

"Now we've got to contend with this drama until he leaves for the day," Alex says. "You have a whole team for you to bounce your ideas off of. There's no reason for you to be so chaotic."

"I'm sorry, you're right. I'll fix this." Samara runs around the table, collecting the copies and placing them in a neat pile. "I just went into a research spiral. I'll get back on track."

The next two hours she plays around with words and delivers to Antonio the new version, after having a couple of people read over her work.

"Here you go, Antonio," she says. Samara hopes invoking his name will help her cause, remind him of how familiar they were with each other not so long ago. She stands as he pulls out a pen and reads. He scratches out sentences and gives it back to her, not once meeting her eyes.

Do better, Samara says to herself while she corrects the mistakes he pointed out and emails the updated version to everyone.

Do better. Do better. Do better.

Her sense of dread never leaves her, even when she's smiling at her co-workers, pretending all is well.

Because of her deep fear of walking past the red door, her delay in leaving her office makes her late to the family lunch. Samara enters the cafeteria to find there's barely any room for her at the table. She stands there holding a pathetic salad, hoping someone would wave her in, but no one does, not Tommy or Alex. Not even Lisa. Samara is relegated to squeezing in at the far end.

When Antonio arrives, everyone begins the dance Samara's been a part of countless times. They tell the designer stories, try to capture his attention and make him laugh. Tommy recounts a night of excess. Lake talks about a celebrity who may or may not be a drug addict. Someone else dishes about a designer from a major fashion house who is about to get fired. All the tales are presented to get the teller into Antonio's good graces, but also to make him forget about the morning's meeting and Samara's implosion. A dysfunctional family ignoring the struggling stepdaughter.

Samara thinks of cutting in, of adding a story of her own. Maybe about the banging on the Library door, and the singing. Or the one about the woman with blood dripping from her hands as she walked down an empty street. No. She doesn't have anything to contribute because all she can think of is Piedad.

"Samara. Hello, Samara."

The sound of her name draws her back to the present.

"What are you going to wear to the dinner?" Lake asks, trying to get her to be part of the conversation. Samara's so grateful for this kind gesture she almost cries.

"I'll be wearing something sexy and salacious, like all of Antonio's designs," she says. "Provocation is what he does best, right?"

She's kissing ass, and everyone knows it, but Antonio nods at the obvious display, so it must be working. The talk then shifts to how much fun the dinner will be and what everyone is planning to wear. Antonio leaves and the rest of the workers finish their lunches. Samara joins in when she can while her mind continues to spiral.

As she gets up, she notices an empty space on the wall. The photo of The Tailor is missing. The same picture Samara stared at right before the lights turned off.

Samara's so scared.

"What happened to the photograph that used to be here?" she asks, pointing to the wall.

Lisa ignores her question and says, "The publicist is waiting for your response to that email she sent earlier."

Samara hurries back to her office. She can't keep failing.

CHAPTER 23

Samara arrives early to work, so early that the only parked cars are of the seamstresses. She can never beat the seamstresses.

Before entering the office she swallows two caffeine pills and drinks her vodka-coffee concoction. Samara spent the long weekend shaming herself and obsessing over how much Antonio thinks she's an idiot. She tried to offset the remorse-spiral with alcohol, which led to ugly vomiting sessions. The caffeine pills are her new way of fighting off hangover sludge. She wears a Mota leather blazer and a sheer skirt and platform boots. The plan is to only wear the designer's clothes from here on out.

Samara also aims to be prompt from now on, chime in at every meeting, answer all emails like a pro. There's nothing she won't do to be a team player. Everyone around her will be satisfied that whatever was bothering her last week will no longer rear its ugly head. The industry likes messiness, but not amongst their own. No one wants to see or hear Samara's drama, so she'll work as hard as she can to conceal it.

"Good morning," she says to the seamstresses, who are not working yet. They sip their cups of coffee, unable to hide their surprise in seeing her in the office at this hour.

"You're here so early!" Rosa exclaims.

"Trying to get a head start," Samara says. "How was your weekend?"

She's very aware that the archives closet is right behind her, breathing down her neck, but she keeps her grin plastered on her face. She nods along as Rosa recounts her Saturday spent at a family gathering.

"And you? What did you do this weekend?" Rosa asks. "Something fun I bet. A party?"

"I didn't do much. Just catching up on work," she says. "There's so much to do. Right?"

The pills must be hitting because Samara's heart is hammering so hard it is outside of her chest. Dolores clears her throat and takes off the protective cloth covering her sewing machine.

Being the perfect worker also means trying once again to get in good with Dolores.

"Did you do anything special this weekend, Dolores?" Samara asks.

"We went to church," she says. As usual, her sour expression never breaks. "We all did."

Rosa rolls her eyes, but Samara is the only one who catches it.

"I should join you next time," Samara says, knowing full well she would never. The only religion she needs to believe in is that she's right where she's meant to be, that Vernon was the correct choice, the only choice. "Light a candle for me next time you're there."

"I will." It sounds more like a threat than a promise but

Samara still thanks her before leaving the group to their coffee and chatter. The seamstresses still remind her of Abuela Lola, and anxiousness fills her body every time Samara thinks about her. Samara subconsciously taps her bag, reassured that the scissors are there.

She unlocks her office door and walks in. It smells stuffy, like dried flowers in stale water. Samara wishes she could open a window and let fresh air in. She places her grandmother's scissors in their usual spot. They're the one constant in her work life.

When she sits at her desk, ready to turn on her computer, that's when she sees it. The picture, waiting for her. The missing photo from the cafeteria wall, no longer in its frame.

Her first reaction is fear, but the emotion is quickly replaced with anger. Someone is playing a cruel trick, trying to trip her up, but they're not going to win.

"Who put this here?" She storms out. "Did someone leave this on my desk?"

The seamstresses squint their eyes and shake their heads, confused as to what Samara's talking about.

"Did you see someone go into my office?" She's trying hard not to sound hysterical or angry, to hold back how she really feels, that she's in a crumbling state of being.

"I didn't see anyone," Rosa says. "Your door was closed when I came in. Right, Dolores?"

Dolores walks over to Samara and looks at the photo. "This belongs in the cafeteria." Her tone of voice hints at Samara taking it, which only enrages her more.

"Yes, I know that. It was missing on Friday and now someone left it on my desk," she says. "Why would anyone do that? Is it supposed to be some kind of a joke?"

Dolores stares at the photo but doesn't touch it. "None of the seamstresses are playing games with you, Samara."

The woman speaks to her like she's a hurt child. Tommy strolls into the office wearing his headphones but tries to do an about-face when he sees Samara barreling toward him.

"This photo, Tommy," she says, blocking his way. "Why would someone leave this in my office?"

"Girl, what are you talking about?" He's over her, but Samara needs answers.

"Is someone playing games? It's not funny," she says. "This photo was missing from the cafeteria the other day and now it's on my desk. Who did this?"

"I've never seen that photo before. Never."

"What? It hangs on the cafeteria wall. It's been there since I started working here," she says. Is everyone in on this? Are they all trying to gaslight her? "Look, it's fucking old."

"Like I said, I've never seen that. Nobody is going into your office. No one is playing games," he says. "You need to chill."

"I need to chill? Someone is messing with me!" She raises her voice and a couple of workers come out, searching to see who is making such a commotion. Tommy gently walks her back to her office and closes the door behind him.

"I'm going to be real with you," he says with a calm voice he rarely uses. "I don't know if you're dealing with something at home or have some personal issues, but no one is trying to get you, and even if they were, a photo? There are easier ways to get someone fired. But what you're doing? Bothering the seamstresses, falling behind on your deadlines? Now those things for sure will get Antonio noticing. Do you understand what I'm saying?"

"Yeah, but—" Samara still holds the picture up.

"No one has time for this," Tommy says. "If you can't handle working here, just quit. It's not that deep."

The mention of leaving her job causes a panic to swell so

great inside of her, made all the worse by the caffeine pills. Resigning is the last thing she wants to do.

"You're right. It's not that deep," she says but doesn't believe her own words.

"Here." He digs into his messenger bag and pulls out a small case filled with gummies. "Eat half of this and just relax."

Samara does what he says and takes a bite of the edible.

"I'm going to be so relaxed, I'll probably be in a coma," she says and Tommy chuckles, which is what she needs. She needs him to believe her. "Thank you."

After he leaves, Samara examines the photo again. *Piedad.* She shakes her head at the woman in the photograph, an imaginary conversation playing in her head, one she refuses to engage in.

The seamstresses eye her as she steps out. Samara holds her breath when she passes the red door of the Library and walks directly to the cafeteria. The space where the photo once hung is still empty. Samara uses a thumbtack to place it back.

CHAPTER 24

THE NEXT DAY when Samara returns to work, the photo is back on her desk, like it never left. Her whole body tenses, and she wants to scream with every fiber in her bones, but Samara forces herself not to react. She fears she's being watched by the person or persons who placed the snapshot there. They expect her to lose it like she did yesterday but Samara refuses to give them the satisfaction. Instead, she goes about starting her day. She puts her bag down, turns on her computer, sets her cup of coffee in its normal place. This is a performance to show whoever is out there that she will not bend.

But the photo *is* there, just begging for her to look at it, and she does. Samara slowly picks it up and examines it. The corners of the picture are slightly curled from age. It even smells old. She flips the image around to find "1910" written in faded pencil. The rage she first felt melts away. In its place is a penetrating curiosity. Samara searches for a hard copy of the ad campaign that will soon run in a weekly magazine. She places the two images next to each other. It's uncanny. The woman in the photo and the woman in the campaign both have the same haunting expression, the same look of deep longing. The same dark eyes. Piedad.

"What are you staring at?"

Alex unexpectedly breaks Samara's concentration.

"Nothing," she says, quickly covering the photo with her hand. "What's up?"

"Want to meet about the brand partnerships?" Alex asks. Her eyes glance over the contents on Samara's desk.

"Sure. Let's do it," Samara says and grabs the items, making sure to keep the photo tucked between some magazines.

"Hey Alex, do you remember the model we used from Consuelo's Farmhouse? Did we ever find her contact information?"

"No, I don't think so. Why?"

"I just thought it would be nice to include her when we cast for the show," Samara says. "Don't you think?"

"Well, she's right across the street. How hard would it be to find her? Just email our contact. Anyway, I was looking at your report on the recent partnerships and I have some thoughts . . ."

Samara goes about the meeting and other work tasks, always performing her role as the best employee, but in the back of her mind she keeps thinking of Piedad. Her rep at the slaughterhouse said she needed a last name to help find her. *She must be here somewhere!* the woman writes, ending the email with a funny face emoji that Samara finds obnoxious.

Throughout the day, she takes glimpses of the photo like she's taking hits of a drug.

"I have a meeting with a new jewelry brand," Samara later announces to her team. "I'll be back online tonight."

She leaves work early and stands in front of Consuelo's Farmhouse to watch the factory workers end their workday.

Samara scans every person, hoping to see Piedad. The longer she waits, the more anxious she feels. An hour goes by. Another. Samara stands still as a statue, waiting for the woman to appear to her again like she did the day of the photo shoot, seemingly out of nowhere.

"Samara!" Rosa yells from the passenger seat of Dolores's car. It must be past five o'clock. "Are you waiting for a ride?"

"I forgot something at work. I'm going home now." Dolores examines her. The seamstress is catching her in a lie, but Samara holds firm. "See you tomorrow."

Because she doesn't want to deal with any more questions, Samara waves goodbye and walks to the end of the street, away from Dolores and her prying eyes. A few streets over, Samara suddenly stops.

She finds herself in front of the church and the construction site. Scaffolding covers the area, but Samara can still make out the shape of the former tailor shop. The facade of the old building was still kept with the newer structure taking shape behind it. Garbage is strewn everywhere, intermingling with the dry leaves blanketing the ground. The only hint that the place isn't completely abandoned is the cheerful sign alerting everyone that Whole Foods will soon be coming. It's funny how her steps landed her back here.

A flimsy gate surrounds the site, but it doesn't take long for Samara to find an opening. She peels open the hole and ducks her head in, careful to avoid catching her outfit on the scaffolding.

"Hello?" she calls out, not wanting to startle any unhoused person. There's no sound, only the rustling of the branches on the dying trees.

Samara pulls out the old photo and holds it in front of her. She can make out the past, can almost see the curtains being pulled back, a face peering out.

Did the woman in the picture want to be in the center of the photo and not hidden? What must it have been like to work in The Tailor at the start of her young life? What happened to her? And what the hell does any of this have to do with Samara?

She picks up a fallen branch and sweeps away some of the dirt. Lost in thought, she uses the tip of the stick and writes out the name *Piedad*. She keeps writing the name over and over, finding different ways of marking the place without really thinking about why she feels compelled to do so. Crouched down to the ground, she writes the name in big letters, in script form, graffiti-style. There's something very calming in the repetition. Samara's obsession is tied to this name, and it's led her here to where The Tailor once stood. There are so many unanswered questions swirling in her mind.

A whiff of the Vernon perfume starts to reach her. Samara crinkles her nose, and yet she doesn't stop writing *Piedad*. The disgusting smell is about to invade the area like a wave of toxic stench, but for whatever reason, she can't leave just yet. There has to be something more, a sign. The smell grows stronger and stronger so she holds her breath and tries not to inhale. She continues to draw the name in the dirt. Hundreds of names surround her. A circle of *Piedads*.

"Excuse me, Miss. You're not supposed to be here."

Startled, she drops the stick. A security guard from Consuelo's Farmhouse calls to her from behind the gate, flashing a light on her face. "This place is off-limits, Miss."

Samara recognizes him. Although the security guard is employed by the slaughterhouse, he's always walking around the neighborhood like a beat cop patrolling the streets.

"Oh, I thought I saw a cat and wanted to make sure it was okay," Samara says. "I heard it meowing."

"There are a lot of cats around here. I don't feed them and neither should you."

"Sorry, I got caught up in something," she says.

The smell is stronger with each step she takes toward the man. Samara covers her nose. The odor stings her eyes.

"I almost called the cops. I saw you earlier walking around." His gray hairs are neatly combed. Not one strand out of place. "The cats aren't going to save you when the building falls on you."

The guard holds open the gate for her and she ducks her head to get through. She takes one more look back at the construction site, almost expecting to see a face looking back at her from somewhere inside.

LATER IN HER APARTMENT, Samara stares at the photo like it will reveal some sort of clue. Hours escape her. The obsession is eating her up, so she inserts the photo between the pages of a magazine and shuts it in the bathroom. She'll spend the rest of the night expecting the bathroom door to open and the image to come to life.

What she needs to do is find Piedad and end this whole compulsion. Samara will see how she's not at all like the woman in the photo, that the factory worker is just that—a regular person who comes in to work, wears a uniform, and slaughters pigs.

Her first thought is of asking Brandon about her, but she quickly drops that idea. No one connected to her work life should be involved in this search. There's no need to have her co-workers question where her mind is at, or for Antonio to find out and add another mark against her. No, she'll talk to someone who "is Vernon."

CHAPTER 25

MARISA SOL WORKS on a large canvas. Her hair is up in a messy bun and her Dickies coverall is splattered with black paint. Oldies play quietly in the background. A sketch of a disembodied woman slowly takes shape under her brush.

"Hope I'm not interrupting." The pills speed everything up, so when Samara speaks the words jumble together, but she's getting used to it. Samara believes the pills and alcohol cancel each other out. To level her trembling hands, she keeps them in the pocket of her leather jumpsuit. Her mind might be glitching, but no one will be able to tell from the way she's dressed—fashion is always there to neutralize any internal drama.

Samara took a chance coming to the gallery. She didn't think the place would be open. No matter what, she needs to get to work on time, but this early morning detour is important. It's all she can think about.

"Good morning," Marisa says, grabbing a wet rag to clean some of the paint off her fingers.

"How are you doing? Are you working on something new?" Samara finds she can't stop jabbering, the words flowing like water from an open hydrant.

"Yes, I'm working." Marisa is annoyed by Samara's unexpected visit and is not invested in hiding it. "Can I help you?"

Samara notices how Marisa has her own eccentric ways too, giving her a what-the-fuck look, but she commits to proceeding anyway. Her shoes loudly clack across the studio.

"I promise not to take up too much of your time. I have to be at work soon but I was hoping you might be able to help me."

Samara pulls out the hard copy of the ad campaign and shows it to Marisa. She doesn't take out the old photo of Piedad, although it's right in her tote.

"I feel like you know everyone in Vernon. Maybe you know or have seen this woman before."

Marisa puts the rag away and takes hold of the page. She pauses for a few seconds and Samara clocks her reaction, trying to locate a hint at what is going through her mind. Recognition? Horror? But she's poker-faced.

"Yeah, she looks familiar."

Samara can't believe it. She didn't expect it to be that simple. "You do? Who is she? I think her name is Piedad and she told me she works at Consuelo's Farmhouse, but I don't think that's true."

"Wow. I bet a lot of money was spent creating this photo shoot," Marisa says. "So how much did Antonio pay her for being his model?"

Samara is embarrassed by the question. She wasn't aware this was going to be an interrogation on labor. "She was compensated with trade. Everyone who worked on the shoot was."

"I heard from workers who did your little fashion shoot.

They got clothes, a dress they probably will never wear. Some were grateful for it though."

Marisa carefully folds the magazine page and returns it to Samara. There's no anger in what she's saying. No malice. She's just relaying facts. Samara can only stand there and take it. What can she possibly say? There's shame she doesn't want to acknowledge. This moment is demanding self-examination, but Samara only wants answers from Marisa.

"Do you know her?"

Marisa pauses before answering. The lull feels too long, especially while Samara's heart is pounding out of sync.

"Wait here," Marisa says and goes to the back room. When she returns, she holds a small canvas. Piedad stares back at Samara from a simple sketch made in pencil. There's no doubt. It's the same person.

"Every year, I host an open house where the community can get their portraits done and pay what they can. It's an exercise for me. Quick five-minute sketches," she says. "And every year, she comes, sits in this chair right here, and lets me capture her likeness. But she never accepts the finished drawing."

"So you know her. Do you have a way of contacting her?"

Marisa shakes her head. "I didn't say I know her. I said she sits there and lets me draw her."

"But who is she?" Samara doesn't hide her desperation. She doesn't know how to, not in front of Marisa, who seems too real to her, too fully in her body. A person who doesn't care for masks or utilizing a fake white voice. Marisa reminds her of her friends back in Jersey, the ones she hasn't spoken to in-depth for months.

"I'm not trying to hurt her. I just want to . . ." Her voice trails off. She can't even finish the sentence because she doesn't know what she would say to Piedad if the woman were standing right in front of her. Would Samara show her the old photo and ask her if she's related to the person?

Would she ask if Piedad is the one haunting her nights?

"You ever thought maybe some people just want to be seen and not forgotten?" Marisa asks.

"I had this idea that she would like to be in the fashion show."

Marisa's laugh is ugly and piercing.

"You're really blind, aren't you? You think someone from a low-paying factory job only wants some overpriced outfit?" she asks. "That's the problem with people like you. You think your job is going to save you. The only thing a corporation wants from you is blood. You can't assimilate into their world. They only want to use your body until you're hollowed out like a husk."

Samara doesn't understand why Marisa is so against the Mota brand. Antonio's not bad, not the way Marisa paints him or the company. Besides, it's just a job.

"Why do you hate Antonio so much? The designer loves Vernon. It's why he set up his company here and why he's doing this fashion show," Samara says. "Besides, we all have to eat. Aren't you painting your broken women for a fee so that some random person, probably a white person, can hang it up on their wall?"

Marisa glares at Samara, then sneers. "Did you ever ask who supports your favorite designer? Where does he get his money? Who's paying your salary?"

"Maybe the reason why you're so angry at Antonio is because he's successful at what he does," Samara says. "He's a legend and is just as much Vernon as you are."

Marisa places the sketch of Piedad down and without warning closes the gap between them. She's so uncomfortably close that Samara keeps moving back until she's up against a wall.

"What the fuck?" Samara asks, chuckling to disguise how much she's afraid. Marisa's eyes are unforgiving, piercing right through her. It was a huge mistake coming here but it's too late. She's trapped while Marisa crowds her, a finger pointing at her face.

"Let me give you a word of advice, Latina to Latina," Marisa says. "Zora Neale Hurston once said not every skinfolk is kinfolk. Do you understand what I'm saying? Wake up."

"Yup, I understand," Samara says, vigorously nodding. "Thanks for your time. I have to go now."

She peels herself off the wall with Marisa only giving her a sliver of space for her to slip through.

"I'll make sure to send you an invite to the show," she says, rushing to the exit. The paintings of dismembered women face Samara, the only witnesses to the artist's threatening stance.

"If Piedad comes around, I'll make sure to let her know you're looking for her," Marisa says as Samara races out of the gallery.

CHAPTER 26

JANUARY 29

TWO WEEKS UNTIL THE FASHION SHOW

A SEVEN-FOOT-TALL IMAGE of a model wearing an Antonio Mota gown waves at Samara like a freakish nightmare. The model morphs into monstrous poses, squatting down on all fours then shooting up tall and gangly, her gown billowing around her spindly body from unseen gusts of wind. The giant apparition flickers on and off, making the semitransparent figure all the more ghastly. She reaches out to Samara with greedy fingers.

"As you can see, the hologram will appear here." The fashion show's producer, Jonathan Augustin, points to a blueprint covering a long wooden table while the giant hologram replays her positions in a garish continuous loop. Samara hates it but her job is not to offer up her opinion or fears. Samara's job is to placate Antonio.

"It's amazing," she says, not looking up at the monstrous model, committing only to facing the producer and her boss. Her grin looks as disturbing as the hologram.

"I don't want to duplicate what's been done," Antonio says. His face is angled toward the cameraman hired to document the making of his big comeback. The film crew captures behind-the-scenes moments of the making of a runway show, a self-funded venture Antonio insisted on. They've been filming for the past three hours and Samara is blessed to be included—evidence of her importance.

"It's not. Don't forget, the audience is going to be listening to Excelia," Samara says. "It's going to be so powerful."

Adding Excelia was Samara's idea. Securing the poet to write new work inspired by the collection cost the company a lot more money than they expected. Ever since Excelia was name-dropped on Beyoncé's last album, the poet has been sought after. Her people kept suggesting that other fashion brands wanted her too, but she was willing to take the job because of how much she loved Antonio. When Samara relayed the message back to the designer, he told her to do whatever it took to secure the poet.

With the fashion show only a couple of weeks away, construction has begun on the set pieces, which are meant to look one part *Blade Runner,* one part California frontier. Dirt floors and wooden encampments will be erected soon for models to drag long leather purses designed to look like rifles. Tommy earlier made a joke about how the models should start lifting weights now before they walk the runway, what with the heavy rifle-purses they'll have to carry around.

"Samara, can you say that again, but this time look up at the hologram?" the director says, while motioning for the cameraman to get a different angle.

"Sure," Samara says, even though she hates looking at the giant.

"Let's be quick about this," Antonio says. He keeps touching his forehead, his face refreshed from another round of Botox. His expression cemented in anger. Antonio may act like he hates being filmed, but Samara can see how desperately he needs the attention. How he hungers to be remembered. Samara can only imagine what Marisa Sol would think of this spectacle, how right her words were to her back in the gallery.

"Why don't we take a break, then?" the director asks.

The hologram is turned off and Samara can breathe a little freer, knowing the giant is no longer lurking above, waiting to crush her.

In the restroom she pops two more caffeine pills. She's been sleeping for only a couple of hours a night, and so has been able to bypass the strange visions. But now her waking life is off-kilter. There are moments when she swears she hears her co-workers cursing her out only to realize they're simply calling her name, or she misreads an email subject line, thinking it has some weird cryptic message sent from beyond only to notice she's way off on her assessment. Her eyes and ears keep playing tricks on her, so she walks around unsure about everything but pretending all is well.

She quit trying to find Piedad because of her run-in with Marisa—doesn't want to even think about the photo. To make sure she stops obsessing over it, Samara placed it in an envelope, sealed it, and left it in the bottom of her office drawer, underneath a pile of magazines.

There are indentations on the inside of her cheeks from clenching her jaw so tight. Throughout the day, her tongue flicks at the bite marks.

"You look so pretty today," Rosa says entering the restroom.

Samara's losing weight and because of this, the praise from everyone has been constant. If she's thin then she must be well too. What her co-workers rave about doesn't connect with the unrecognizable reflection staring back at her. The Samara before her is disappearing, a shell of her former self, but at least the diluted version is worthy of recognition from others.

"Um, Samara, I know you're super busy, but have you had a chance to ask around if anyone is looking to hire?" Rosa asks. She too has changed. Her transformation from mousy, green innocent to budding ingenue is almost complete. She is way more intentional with the clothes she wears. Rosa's still a little off in her style, but anyone can recognize she's gathering her recent fashion insights from her co-workers, especially Samara. Today she wears a denim top and pencil skirt with an oversized black blazer that's definitely a thrift find.

"Sorry, I've been really busy," Samara says.

"No, I totally understand," she says. "Everything is so crazy right now. Just keep me in mind."

"Of course." Samara hates brushing her off. Rosa has a sweetness she finds endearing. It's a quality many in the industry would love to bottle and market.

"I'd better get back," Rosa says. "We're celebrating Señora Lopez's birthday today."

She watches Rosa return to Seamstress Row. A single candle is lit on a small cupcake and placed in front of Señora Lopez. The elderly seamstress has been at the company just as long as Dolores. They're identical in weird ways. A sweater always draped across their shoulders. A stern motherly composure.

When Rosa joins the group, she avoids standing by Dolores, but the seamstress still manages to find her. Dolores brushes against Rosa but she moves away from the unwanted touch. The slight is triggering to watch. Samara's jaw clenches tightly as she walks back outside.

The crew films for another couple of hours. She avoids eye

contact with the giant apparition and does her best to deliver the lines fed to her. Samara is happy when it's over and she no longer feels the video monster breathing on her.

"Samara, walk with me."

Alex makes a move to join them, but Antonio puts his hand up to stop her. A thrill surges through Samara. It feels like ages since Antonio has confided anything in her. Instead, he's been leaning on the producer or Tommy or anyone else he's christened his current fave.

"I don't trust Jonathan and I want you to make sure he does what I ask," he says conspiratorially. "He's going to make me look like an idiot."

"I'll make sure your notes are implemented," Samara says, although she has literally nothing to do with it.

"Also, go over the guest list with what's-her-name." Antonio picks off a piece of lint from the Mota blouse Samara wears and gives her a nod of approval. He likes what he sees, likes how she's losing weight and her face is gaunt and scary like the hologram's. At least it's fashion, and Antonio is paying attention. "I don't want to be seated by anyone I hate."

"I'll go over the guest list today and play around with the seating arrangements," she says, her smile so extreme it breaks open the cuts in her mouth. "I will take care of it. It's going to be so great!"

Antonio doesn't thank her. He just tells one of his assistants to follow him back in. Samara swallows the metallic taste of blood and enjoys the moment. This is good. The designer trusts her. She's back in the favored circle.

"What did he want?"

Not too long ago Alex, Lake, and the others were steering clear of Samara and her stench of failure, but one private meeting with Antonio and all that changes.

"Nothing, just wants me to go over the guest list. Lake, do you have the current RSVPs?" she asks.

"Do you want my input?" Alex asks. There's a hint of desperation. Samara feels vindicated enough to relish it.

"Sure, the more the merrier," she says. "Let's go to the conference room to fix this seating chart." Samara is in charge. She's back to leading.

"Hey, Lake, will you take care of Rosa, save her from Dolores and the church ladies?" Samara asks. "She's looking to make a move."

"She's already spoken to me. Don't worry. I'll find something for her to do." Lake playfully bumps into Samara. "We have to look out for each other. Right?"

The only thing that matters is how Antonio's back to confiding in Samara. She may no longer have a fat Cuban ass to fall back on—not when she's gotten so thin her bones are protruding back there—but at least she has her boss's love once again.

CHAPTER 27

SAMARA ADJUSTS HER nipple cover, then sips a glass of champagne. Her phone blows up with people begging to score an invite to tonight's dinner, but she's not responding. With the artist Villano Antillano performing, the invite-only dinner has become the event of the night. The music was a last-minute addition, a suggestion Samara helped to secure. Pre–fashion show buzz is what Antonio wants and Villano has delivered just that.

"Glow," Samara instructs the makeup artist working on her face. "I want to glow."

"You're going to look like a shooting star." The makeup artist applies gold chrome flakes on Samara's eyelids. "The world will go blind."

Everyone is on deck to work tonight, but that doesn't mean she has to look like crap while doing so. But there's no question that no matter how she appears on the outside, Samara feels like shit on the inside.

"Oh my god, I love it!" exclaims Lisa once the makeup artist is done with Samara's face. The approval from people at work only adds to the illusion that everything is fine.

"Here you go." Lisa delivers a form-fitting dress from the archives, helping her to once again avoid the Library. When no one is looking, Samara flips the garment inside out and checks for the name Piedad but it doesn't appear anywhere.

There's a delicate dance she performs where she appears to be in total control of her surroundings. But the opposite is in effect. There's absolutely no control. She's cosplaying as a person who isn't afraid, who is put together, able to function in stressful situations. It's not difficult to do this when you're a ghost of yourself, slowly fading away.

"Let's go!" Tommy yells.

Samara grabs a clutch. There's no room for Abuela Lola's scissors in the tiny bag and she hates leaving them behind. Protection is what she needs, but she has no choice. Fashion always prevails. She joins Tommy, Alex, and the fashion show producer, Jonathan, in the idle car waiting to take them to Olivia Celis's mansion, making one stop first to pick up an emerging starlet. Everyone looks fly as fuck, glistening with sexuality and confidence. Samara too. She blends in while her insides churn.

"Want some?" Jonathan offers a line of coke and one by one, her co-workers take a hit. This is her first time doing this in front of them, but not her first time doing coke. She tried it back in college, but it was never her thing; not the way alcohol is. When it's her turn, Samara hesitates for a second, but not long enough to change her mind. Those in the car are doing it and she'll follow along, a team player to the very end. *We accept you. You're one of us.*

SOMETHING ABOUT THE CELIS HOUSE is different. The place is not as stilted as before, with the museum-like quality replaced by a welcoming charm. There are floral arrangements everywhere, giving off a sweet aroma of jasmine and lilies. The dinner is being held outside in the vast backyard with heating lamps already fired up. Holding court at the far corner is Olivia Celis, looking like royalty in one of Antonio's designs.

Samara's chest tightens, which could be the coke mixing in her bloodstream or the anxiousness of seeing the old woman again. Olivia's sordid Vernon history is somehow tied to Antonio, and that means she's also tied to Samara's future. And so she must kiss the ring.

"Ms. Celis, it's great to see you again," she says. "The place looks immaculate."

Olivia squints at her, trying to place the face. After a couple of beats she recognizes Samara and gives her an awkward hug.

"Sandra, right?"

"No, my name is Samara." Her thoughts shift to violent visions of what she would like to do to this woman—squeeze her wrinkly throat until she stops breathing. Beat her while asking her if she ever thinks about the workers who died in her family's factories. The dark thoughts leave Samara almost breathless but she keeps talking, the need to be liked by the woman outweighing the hatred.

"It's such a great turnout," Samara says. "Thank you for hosting."

"Oh, this?" Olivia shoos the notion away. "I would do anything for Antonio. He brings so much vitality to Vernon. A successful designer who gives back, always thinking about his community."

"Yes, he's a great mentor to many," Samara says, following along. The small talk continues like they're both reading off the same script.

Olivia's assistant comes over and tells her something for her ears only. Suddenly, the old woman's face radiates as if a heavenly beam of light has been bestowed on her.

"I was told I would find the most beautiful women at this party standing right here, and they were right."

The familiar voice approaches and Samara suddenly feels uneasy. She follows Olivia's loving gaze to Brandon, who walks toward them holding a cocktail in each hand and wearing a velvet suit in black. So much has transpired since Samara last saw him. She feels vulnerable in front of him but conceals it well.

"You evil boy." Olivia sounds like a young woman. Her voice is flirty and high-pitched. Brandon plants a kiss on her cheek.

"It's good to see you, Samara." Brandon does the same to her, but his kiss lingers. His mischievous grin reminds her how much she still wants to fuck him. But his appearance also reignites a fear buried so deep inside that she wonders if she's confusing fear with excitement.

"*You* know Brandon?" Olivia sounds annoyed. Brandon must be her little treasure, and not for Sandra or Samara—or whatever she thinks her name is—to share.

"Everyone knows Brandon," Samara says. "Isn't he practically the mayor of Vernon?"

"Brandon is very good at discovering talent and alerting me to new ventures. The arts, culture. He's always been the first to tell me who I should be paying attention to," Olivia says. "It's a family trait. The Celises are great connectors."

"A family trait?" Samara asks, confused. She must have heard her wrong.

"Sí, soy su nieto favorito," he says. Brandon grabs Olivia's hand. "¿No es cierto, abuela?"

"Yes, you are my favorite boy," the woman says.

Samara hides her surprise with a fake smile.

CHAPTER 28

BRANDON COOS AT his grandmother and the matriarch laps up the attention, beaming like a child receiving candy. They continue to love up on each other while Samara takes in the sudden family reunion.

"I didn't know you were related," she says.

"Yes. I stopped using Celis when I went to college," Brandon says. "Too many people accused me of being a nepo baby before that was even an expression."

Now that she thinks about it, she can see the resemblance. It can be found by the way the Celises examine things and people, with such an intense curiosity, branding what's useful to them and discarding what isn't. Olivia and Brandon are also very charming, but the old woman only allows a select group to see that side of her, unlike her grandson, who is way more generous with his charisma.

Another thing the two of them share is that they attract the admiration of everyone around them. This dinner may be technically honoring Antonio, but the guests are much more interested in Brandon and Olivia—what they're doing right at this moment, who they're speaking to. Those invited came because they wanted to be near the Celises, to get their attention. And because of her proximity to them via Antonio, Samara finds herself beloved by association. This is what she's always wanted—to be seen—so she leans into the attention and ignores the dread inching up her spine.

"You should never hide who you really are," Olivia says to Brandon. The flash of anger so familiar to Samara rears its head. "You're a Celis."

"Of course I am." Brandon tries soothing his grandmother's temper. "Now let's not get worked up about it. I'm not denying where I'm from."

"Don't you ever forget it," she says. "We are more Vernon than Vernon."

Samara experiences déjà vu, but a bell announces that dinner will be served and gives her the respite of not having to examine the thought.

"Allow me." Brandon extends his arms to both women, offering to escort them to their seats. When they reach the main table, a person from Olivia's team quickly leads her to Antonio.

Updating the seating chart had been one of Samara's priorities. She made sure to leave a professional distance between her and Brandon. But when he realizes the arrangement, he doesn't let her go to her assigned table.

"There must be a mistake," he says. "There's no way you're sitting so far away from me."

"It's fine. We can catch up after dinner."

Samara notices Antonio clocking this interaction. Brandon is even more off-limits to her now that she's been made aware of his family's importance to the brand. Samara can't jeopardize her current good standing with the designer, especially when it's dangling by the thinnest of threads.

"Antonio, you're looking good," Brandon says, giving her boss a hug. "Are you ready for the big show? Everyone can't stop talking about it."

"It's all thanks to you and your family," Antonio says. "This is all so touching. Olivia shouldn't have gone through all the trouble."

"We're proud of you," Brandon says. "Besides, the family only backs winners. Right, abuela?"

Olivia is too busy being photographed to respond. Samara tries to leave, but Brandon pulls her in for a photo.

"The best thing you did this past year was bring Samara into the fold," Brandon says to Antonio. "The brand needed new blood."

Samara shrugs off Brandon's exaggerated take, especially when Antonio can't hide his disdain for it. He hates anyone taking credit for any of his accomplishments, but Antonio also can't afford to shun his sponsor. He stares at Samara, waiting for her to correct Brandon's impression.

"You're wrong. I'm the lucky one," she says. "I owe Antonio everything."

The bell rings again and a party coordinator urges them to take their seats.

"Brandon, your table is right there," Samara says, eager to take her leave. "Is there anything else I can do?"

His look says it all. She knows what he wants, but this is work, and she's going to keep it professional all the way through.

"Antonio, you don't mind if I borrow Samara for the night?" Brandon asks. "Got some old friends who could use some educating on the fashion world."

Before Samara can even protest, Brandon leads her away.

When they're a safe distance, he whispers, "You're not getting away that easily."

It's a thrill to be wanted, even if Brandon is off-limits. Him wanting her boosts her social currency.

The small group at his table stands to greet her. Brandon introduces her to Kevin Lee, a venture capitalist, Brian Soto, a CEO and founder of a social media app everyone is buzzing about, and Evan Parker, a CEO of a men's beauty brand. They're in their early thirties and dressed in designer clothes, Rolex watches on their wrists and diamond hoops on their ears. Investors and tech bros ready to take over the world—and searching for pretty young things. Their eyes are constantly moving, looking at Mota's employees, or at their model friends, or even ogling Samara.

The conversation jumps from the demise of a tech company to the latest Hollywood movie everyone needs to watch, eventually landing on Vernon. All the while Brandon caters to Samara like she's the guest of honor, making sure her glass is always full and that she's included in every discussion. With each drink, Samara slowly quells the trepidation she'd earlier felt about him, until it's practically gone. Every once in a while, though, she glances over to Antonio and Olivia's table and worries whether she's doing what is expected of her. Tommy said to not be messy. No matter the temptation, she will not fall.

"Where else is there to go?" Brian asks. "Downtown L.A. is dead. We're building Vernon. It's the new frontier."

"The new frontier?" Samara asks with the sweetest expression. Brandon chuckles beside her. "I'm sure those who have called Vernon home since before any of you would like a word or two with you about that."

"Oh, are you one of those?" Kevin asks, laughing.

"One of what?"

He fills her glass before proceeding. "Liberals."

"I'm just not stupid enough to think you can build over a place that already exists," she says, taking the glass.

"This coming from someone who works for a global brand charging thousands of dollars for one dress," Brian says.

"That's why you're here tonight, right? To go shopping?" Samara asks. "Or just trying to find a model to fuck?"

The table erupts in laughter. Samara loves how Brandon showers her with attention even while she's playing this game of one-upmanship with his friends. The dinner is a success *because* of her, because of her wittiness and her brashness.

Because Brandon wants her.

When Villano takes to the stage installed just for their performance, Brandon places his hand on Samara's neck to guide her as they hunt for a better view. The slight brush of his fingers feels good, but she vows she won't fuck him. Not tonight.

"Where have you been hiding?" he asks. "Avoiding me?"

"No, just busy," she says.

Standing by the small stage where Villano raps about her designer pussy is Antonio, with his partner, Steven. Samara counts how many times the designer looks over to them. Her boss is checking on her, making sure she doesn't do anything to embarrass him or to screw with his bag. The Celises are crucial to him, and there's power in knowing that she can do some damage. And Brandon liking her is elevating her status, her importance.

"Let's go somewhere else where we can catch up," Brandon says. And she realizes this is the moment: She can leave with him and forget about everything that happened between them that night, or she can be smart.

"I'm sorry, but I'm on call," she says, waving at Antonio. Steven waves back. "I need to stay focused on the show."

"And I'm distracting you. Don't you want to be distracted?" he jokes, but Samara keeps a straight face. "Okay, I can respect that. I don't like it but I can respect it."

They vibe to the music and he adheres to her wishes for the most part, but it gets harder and harder to stay firm with him. It's confusing what her focus should be.

The event ends promptly at ten and everyone wants to continue partying, including Brandon, but for once Samara says no. She's committed to being the good team player.

"Don't worry about me," she says to the group. "I'll just call a car service."

"There's no way I'm going to let you take a taxi when I can just drive you home," Brandon says.

"You really don't have to."

"Samara, let Brandon take you home," Lake adds. Tommy and the rest agree. "Don't be silly." She can see that her "no" is making the situation worse, so she gives in.

It's dangerous being in a car with him. She isn't strong enough to resist him forever, but the ride is quick. When he leans in and tries to kiss her, she pulls away.

"You're killing me," he moans. "Why are you holding back?"

"It was great seeing you," she says. "I promise, after the show I'll be all yours."

Samara quickly steps out of the car and closes the door before she changes her mind. He flashes that mischievous grin.

In her apartment, she draws the blinds of her windows, making sure her place is nice and dark. She's fucked up but not too fucked up, which is another thing to be proud of.

"Nena mala, no sabes amar." Still wired, she recites Villano's lyrics. What does it mean to want Brandon but also be afraid of wanting him? She combs through her thoughts, trying to reassemble that night they spent together, but she can never

make her memories quite linear. The longer she dwells on it, the easier it becomes for her to change her recollection of that moment. Samara finds she can convince herself of anything, even that the night she spent with Brandon was just a wild, sensuous experience.

She falls asleep quickly, but it won't last long, not when the clock ticks away. It will be two in the morning soon, and the disturbing nightly noises will be joining her shortly.

CHAPTER 29

At exactly two, a heavy rush of heat awakens her. When Samara opens her eyes, a weight presses down on her legs, pinning her body to the mattress. She's unable to move. Not her fingers or her arms. Not her legs.

There's the sound of a grunt, low, like a train rumbling across the city. The windows are shut and the sound is definitely coming from inside her apartment. She wants to run, to get away from whatever is making the noise, but can't. Samara tries to will her body to obey, but she can't even wiggle her toes. She has no strength.

The stench from the slaughterhouse, a deathly mix of sulfur and vomit, causes her to gag. She breathes through her mouth in short bursts. There's not enough oxygen.

A grunt, this one closer to her bed.

"Wake up, bitch," she urges herself. "Wake up."

The thing draws nearer and Samara tries getting up. But her

arms feel strapped to the bed, her head the only part of her moving.

Another grunt. This time it's near her toes. Something has climbed up her bed and under the sheets. She feels alien hairs on her toes and then legs. The beast sniffs at her crotch. It trails on top of her. She is paralyzed, unable to scream or cry. She's stuck. Any slight move and this animal will tear into her.

"Diferente. Soy diferente."

It is not Samara talking to herself. There's someone else in the room. Someone or something lying beside her on the bed. Samara doesn't know where to look, which direction to turn. This thing is trying to kill her, wanting to drag her down to a hell she's never asked to be a part of. This is not meant for her. None of this.

And yet, Samara has to look. She has to.

She slowly turns her head.

A young woman lies beside her. The woman stares at the ceiling, crying. Samara recognizes her right away. It's the same person she saw that night not too long ago, standing in the middle of the street with blood on her hands. The same person in the picture. The same woman she's been obsessing over.

Piedad.

This vision, this ghost, grips Samara's sheets tight, so tight the knuckles on her fingers glow a disturbing white. Samara's bed shakes, and she's unsure whether it's her own fear or that of Piedad that causes it to rattle. The headboard bangs against the wall in a steady rhythm that starts as a tap, then increases in violence.

The beast continues its climb and is now atop Samara's stomach. A warm stream of liquid trickles down her legs. She's peed on herself. The fear is so great.

"God, please, no," Samara whispers. "Please."

Piedad's face is covered in dirt, streaks of tears trailing down to her neck. Her stringy hair is damp, the strands sticking to her cheek. She's so close to Samara. There's nowhere to run. Samara is attuned to everything around her. How an animal nuzzles her breast and how the air seems thick with something poisonous. And that this woman, this apparition, is right beside her. Her pleading eyes reveal that she's just as frightened as Samara. And Samara's so scared her teeth are chattering like the clacking of a typewriter.

She prays to Abuela Lola, for her to save her from this abomination. These evil apparitions circling around her, trying to end her life, while Abuela Lola is busy offering signs to others. Why didn't her grandmother warn her?

Piedad opens her mouth wide, disturbingly wide, until it becomes a large abyss, a hole too big for her frame. Something is inside Piedad's mouth, way down her throat. It slowly crawls out, squirming in the darkness.

Maggots fall from Piedad's mouth. Hundreds of them worm their way out, dangling from her lips. So many now cover the pillow, the sheets. They land by Samara.

The headboard bangs out of control in a frenzy. Maggots cover Piedad. They crawl across both their bodies.

A snort. The sheet slowly lifts. She doesn't want to look down, doesn't want to witness this horror, but she does. Two beady eyes stare back at her. A pig, its snout wet against Samara's breast.

"Diferente."

Piedad is no longer lying beside Samara in the bed. She stands somewhere in the dark and makes whimpering sounds like a dog. Samara convulses from absolute terror.

"What do you want?" she whispers, so afraid of the animal

still nuzzling her chest, its hot breath on her. "What do you want from me?"

The ghost of the woman from that picture, taken so long ago, is standing in the corner of her apartment, crying, and looking very much alive. The pig is real too, its drool covering Samara's neck. She's certain this is how she'll die, frightened to death. She doesn't want to see this, to be a witness to these disturbing visions. This is devil shit, punishment for her past mistakes.

"Please," Samara begs.

The ghost ventures forward. There are no more maggots pouring forth from her mouth. Instead, Piedad's lips are sewn shut, stitches covered in blood. She's frantic but unable to scream. She claws at her cheeks, leaving long scratches. Piedad reaches out to Samara, her dirty fingernails digging into Samara's arm. Her whimpers are the only noise she can make from behind her lips, sewn shut by a single continuous hand-stitched thread.

Unlike Piedad, Samara screams. She flails about, punching the air, the headboard, at the beast, at the tortured woman. Samara screams until she has no voice, until the torment is too much, until everything goes dark.

CHAPTER 30

Samara's prone body lies on the floor of the Library. Her body flinches, battling with her subconscious for control of itself. The archives are in disarray, clothes everywhere, except for a strange arrangement around her. Antonio Mota's gowns are laid on the floor in a circle like flower petals. The dresses, empty shells eager for a body to pour into them.

Samara is so deep in her sleep that she doesn't hear the seamstresses entering the building to start their workday. She doesn't hear the chatting in Spanish, although some words filter into her dream state, and when they do, the voices only cause her body to jerk even more.

The jingling of the keys Dolores uses to open the door also doesn't quite disturb her sleep, but she's slowly realizing that her body feels trapped in mud. Samara whimpers because she's starting to remember.

Only when Dolores enters the Library and gasps at finding

Samara sprawled on the floor does she wake up with a piercing scream. She thrashes around, swinging violently at the pig and the ghost, at anyone who draws near. Samara can't understand how she's not in her apartment anymore, and those visions that attacked her are gone. The seamstresses stream into the Library. They try to calm her down, but Samara is inconsolable. She buries her face in the clothes, trying to make sense of the senseless.

"Is she here?" she cries out.

"Who?" Rosa asks.

"Piedad! The pig!"

"Quick, go get her some water," Dolores says, and Rosa runs out. When she returns, she presses the glass to Samara's lips. Samara allows herself to be lifted up and placed on a chair. Another seamstress fans her lightly with a piece of cardboard. Others slowly put the clothes back on the racks. Samara hears them moving around, but doesn't look at them. Her mind races.

"I don't know how I got here," she eventually says. "I was home. I was dreaming, I think . . . I . . ."

"Déjennos," Dolores says with firmness. The seamstresses leave the room. Rosa hesitates but eventually closes the door behind her.

There's nothing Samara can do to fix whatever this is, this madness that has afflicted her. She tries to get up from the chair and follow the seamstresses out, but her legs give way. Dolores guides her right back to the seat. Outside, the sewing machines purr to life.

"I'm going to say something to you, and I'm not sure if you'll listen, but you must," Dolores begins. She grabs hold of Samara's hands. Samara's taken aback by the woman's sudden kindness. She stares at the thick fingers and the calluses forming on the tips of them, so like Abuela Lola's.

Samara is completely lost. Chunks of time keep vanishing and she can't explain why. How did she end up here? She has no recollection of leaving her apartment. To continue to pretend nothing is happening is stupid, because she's drowning. Her tears land softly atop Dolores's skin and follow the seamstress's wrinkles like a stream flowing down a mountain.

"You're in danger," Dolores says. "These are signs alerting you. If you don't take heed, it won't be the floor where we'll find you next."

"I'm going to stop drinking. I promise," Samara says. "I've been relying on it too much. I can see that now."

Dolores squeezes Samara's hand. Outside, more workers are coming in. Tommy, Lake, others. Someone asks for Samara, wondering where she is.

"It's not the drinking. There is someone evil circling around you," Dolores says.

"Do you mean Piedad?" Samara asks. She looks frantically about, afraid the ghost will return simply by mentioning her name. "Have you seen her too?"

"No, it's not a woman," Dolores says. "Come with us to service. We can help you. With the help of God."

"But you must know! She's the one trying to kill me!" Samara exclaims. Her voice gets louder.

"Samara, listen to me," Dolores says. "Let me take you to our service where we can pray through this. We can help you."

Samara lets go of her hand. Dolores is trying to trick her into attending mass and doesn't give a fuck about what's actually happening to her.

"I'm not going to church. That's not going to help me. No, I'm not doing this." Why is this old woman desperate to lead her into some religious cult like she's some sheep, like she's *Rosa*?

"Please leave me alone," Samara says. "I'm fine."

"No, you're not fine." Dolores's tongue flicks out of her mouth like a snake. Samara bites the inside of her cheek to keep from screaming.

"Um, I was . . ." She takes deep breaths, closes her eyes tight, and starts again. "I came back to the office after dinner to finish up something I was working on and must have fallen asleep here."

The seamstress folds her arms in front of her. The motherly concern she'd shown seconds ago vanishes. She's back to the cold, stern elder Samara met when she first arrived.

"We're going to pray for you," Dolores says, then walks out, leaving Samara alone.

Samara clenches her fingers so tight that when she releases them her nails leave crescent moon markings on her skin. The goal is to place this moment into a box and bury it deep in the crevices of her mind. Samara has become an expert in discarding the questions around her. No need to analyze any of it.

"Samara, is everything okay?" Lake enters the room and closes the door behind her. "Is there something going on between you and Dolores? She can be a little too set in her ways. If you want, I can bring it up to Antonio."

The anatomical heart tattoo on Lake's wrist appears to be beating. As it pulses it lifts her fair skin up and down. Samara can even see blood whooshing through the tattoo heart's ventricles. Lake scratches her arm and blood from the ventricles drips out and down to the floor.

"Your wrist," Samara says, pointing to the blood creating a puddle by Lake's shoes. "It's on the floor."

"Are you feeling sick? Do you need me to call a car to take you home?" Lake asks. "Let me do that."

Samara steadies her breath. She's got to keep it together. She can't afford to fall apart in front of her co-workers.

"I'm sorry," she says. "I just need a moment."

The blood continues to flow out of Lake's wrist. Samara can't take much more of looking at the gory injury, but she grins, the whites of her teeth feeling dry against her lips.

"It's just my period. I get really bad cramps. Can you believe my timing?" she asks. "I can't afford to be sick. Not now."

Lake shifts into help mode. "I can *so* relate. I've got painkillers for that. Sit here and I'll get them. I'll tell the others to give you some space. Okay?"

Blood keeps leaking from Lake's wrist, creating a trail behind her as she leaves the room.

There is nothing going on. You're just overworked, Samara tells herself. *The stress is getting to you.*

She presses her palms together and inhales deeply. Her mind is playing tricks on her. It's making her question her sanity, but Samara's fine. Nothing is wrong. She just has to focus on what's important—on the fashion show and on keeping this job. That's all.

WHEN LAKE RETURNS with the painkillers, there's no more blood flowing out of her wrists. Her tattoo is just that—a tattoo.

"Here you go. They're pretty powerful, so I would take only one."

Settled back in her office, Samara washes down all the painkillers Lake gave her with vodka. She doesn't even bother hiding the bottle; just leaves it out in the open. She asks Lisa to find her a change of clothes to wear and to not disturb her for an hour.

For the rest of the day, Samara drinks and works and drinks. Dolores and the seamstresses no longer address her or make eye contact with her except for Rosa. When Samara walks past the group, Rosa lightly pats her arm, and this simple act Samara holds on to.

"I'VE CHECKED THE TRAPS. There's nothing there, but I've put a call in to the exterminator again," Raul says. "He'll be back here tomorrow morning."

Samara's body is drenched in sweat while she waits for Raul to finish checking her apartment for vermin. She was too afraid to walk in there on her own, unsure of what state her place would be in, but she didn't dare ask anyone from work for help. Instead, she turned to Raul.

"You don't see anything?" she asks from the hallway. "Any weird droppings or maggots? Does it smell?"

"No, nothing," Raul says. "If it's rats, we'll get them."

She cautiously enters. Her bed is made up. No signs of maggots or blood. No smell of urine. Nothing out of the ordinary except for the empty liquor bottles strewn all over the studio.

"Anything else I can do for you?" Raul asks. She sees him noticing the bottles too, and how pity blankets his face. When he leaves, Samara drinks heavily, jumping at the slightest noise.

CHAPTER 31

February 9

One day until the fashion show

It's been raining for the past two days. The unexpected storm has produced torrential downpours and mudslides. Newscasters can't stop stating how unusual the weather is and how the city is not prepared for this amount of water. The runway show is tomorrow, and the threat of cancellation is real, so real that the interns have been asked to monitor the weather apps and report immediately any sign of change, good or bad.

Despite the weather, contractors are outside banging away with their hammers to still finish the outdoor set in time. Their hard hats are wrapped in plastic, but it doesn't do much to protect them from the deluge.

"Jesus Christ," Jonathan says.

The wind has picked up the slaughterhouse stench and deposited it right in front of the producer as he stands huddled under an umbrella in front of the set. His team covers their noses and one crew member even starts to gag. The rain seems to only intensify the odor.

Unlike the producer, Samara is finally used to the Vernon perfume. At least it's familiar, and that is better than she can expect anymore.

Samara imagines the rain never stopping. The clouds growing darker and thicker. The storm existing over only the fashion house. She sees a tidal wave flooding the runway, knocking down the towering models as they slip and slide across the stage. Bodies in beautiful gowns floating down Soto Avenue. Dangling electrical cords landing on the set and electrocuting the models, the makeup artists, the stylists.

Even her.

The wicked thoughts are constant and only seem to get more and more violent and elaborate as the day drags on. *It wouldn't be so bad if they came true,* Samara thinks, *at least then people would talk about Antonio's "great comeback."* Memes would be created. The horrible turn of events would be reenacted on TikTok.

Because besides the rain, the other problem is that there's no clear buzz. The company used their typical playbook, did their best to center Antonio in articles previewing the fashion show. But no one is interested in the story of Antonio's "comeback," no matter how hard his team tries to shake things up. People want to hear only of the new designers.

The expensive publicist he hired was able to snag a feature about Antonio, accompanied by a portrait of him surrounded by the new players in fashion. Antonio hated the photo. He kept saying he looked like an old lady surrounded by "All About Eves"—and he wasn't wrong. If only he'd said something shocking in the interview, because even when he tried to make subtle digs at one of the designers he sounded too much like a fallen king who was upset that his royal subjects no longer cared for him. But time has run out. Tomorrow is the big day.

"What the hell are you doing out there?" With everyone back inside the office, Antonio conferences in from New York, his voice so loud it projects his venom for everyone in The Saprophyte to hear. It's like he's saved his special screams for his Vernon team. "I expect this to work!"

"The alternative is to bring the show indoors," Jonathan says. "Construct a smaller set where Shipping and Receiving is. Maybe utilize the factory. It will give it more of an industrial feel."

"The Vernon show isn't important anyway," Alex whispers to Samara. "What's important is New York."

"You try telling him that," Samara says as she imagines bodies falling off the stage while Antonio is still calling them stupid, accusing them of not knowing a thing.

Why did I even hire any of you?

Samara pulls out a spanking new bottle of vodka and calmly distributes plastic cups. She pours and hands them out to Jonathan and the rest of the team. She drinks hers straight, no chaser. Not even water.

"We'll fix this." Samara manages to squeak the words out of her mouth. She takes another shot while Antonio finds interesting new ways to curse them out. Eventually his voice becomes a drone. "We'll get it done, Antonio. Don't worry about a thing."

She placates him with sweet words until he finally hangs up.

Alex looks like she's about to cry, and Samara should console her, but there's nothing left in her to do so. Everyone is living in their own separate hell and Samara needs all her strength to keep afloat.

"We should start drinking now and never stop," she says.

"Lake, I know you're busy, but we need food. Can you take our delivery order and charge it to our account?"

Her co-workers move quickly around her as they move the show indoors. Everyone yells. No one talks nicely or adds a "please" after any ask. It is all barks and orders, *Fuck you* and *Just get it done*. But as Samara flows in and out of the commotion, she rides this wave of chaos by numbing herself with vodka along the way.

The interns are set up in the cafeteria to fill up swag bags for VIPs. Rosa sits among them. When she sees Samara, Rosa runs up to her.

"Are you busy?" she asks.

"I need to finish a thing." What she's really talking about is finishing the drink she left on her desk.

"I just wanted to tell you quickly: Lake introduced me to Brandon the other day. He said he already has some work lined up for me," Rosa says. She's so excited. "I get to meet with them tomorrow."

At least Rosa is finding a way out of this nightmare. Samara is almost jealous, but tamps the green-eyed monster down. There are way too many other monsters trying to kill her.

"Good! I'm so happy," she says. "I told you it would all work out. You won't have to be here for much longer."

"And you?" Rosa asks, whispering. "How are you feeling?"

"I'm doing great!" Samara leaves her before any other questions arise.

The nightly noises and visions are kept at bay if she keeps her legs and lips moving. Samara feels sure she can outwit these demons trying to drag her down. She jogs back to her office so she can continue to drink this discomfort away, only to find an old friend waiting for her.

The photo of Piedad is back on her desk. Samara could

swear she hadn't taken out the photo, but it doesn't matter. The photo is nevertheless there to keep the nightmare going.

"No," she says in despair. "No, no, no."

She inhales her drink before looking for a box of matches. The box is from the Vernon Speakeasy where she went on the night she hooked up with Brandon.

She lights a match and holds it to the photo. The edge catches on fire. The lick of the flame is tiny but it grows. This simple act of burning the photo is Samara adding to the chaos. Piedad will not be joining her. Not if Samara can help it.

She blows on the flame, helping the smoke rise until the alarms go off. The image of Piedad curls up and becomes black.

"Are you crazy!" Alex runs into her office brandishing a fire extinguisher. A crowd forms outside.

"Sorry!" Samara yells. "I must have left a candle on. I couldn't take the Vernon perfume anymore."

Some of her co-workers giggle, but not Dolores and the seamstresses. Dolores's expression is cold as ever, but there's an undertone of concern behind those eyes that Samara refuses to acknowledge.

"Jesus Christ, Samara!" Tommy yells. "Can you try not to kill us?"

"I'm going to try!" Her laugh doesn't even sound like hers. Someone is using her body like a puppet and moving her lips.

A terrible mark is left on top of her desk after she wipes the ashes away.

"Dolores, you don't mind, do you?"

Samara grabs a long piece of muslin from Dolores's workstation. She doesn't stop her, but Samara can sense the disapproval, the judgment. It's always been there, ever since she started working here. Dolores and her group have always disliked her.

She drapes the fabric across the desk and places Abuela Lola's scissors atop it. Then she keeps on moving, busy as ever. There's no time to think.

Outside, the rain is relentless.

CHAPTER 32

FEBRUARY 10

THE DAY OF THE FASHION SHOW

SAMARA HIDES IN the restroom, afraid to go to her office. If the picture of Piedad appears on her desk she's not sure how she'll react. That might be the end for her. The final break. At least she was smart enough to ask a makeup artist to take care of her before the models or other workers arrived. She's camera-ready and meltdown-ready, but no amount of foundation can mask the chemicals already circulating inside of her . . . and there's still so much room for more concoctions.

"Samara!"

Alex calls to her from somewhere inside the office. Samara can't hide in this bathroom forever.

"The rain is picking up again," Lake announces over the office speakers. *"Everyone's going to die."*

Someone screams in agony.

Samara presses her body against the bathroom door. She closes her eyes and pinches her skin until she flinches from the pain.

"The rain is picking up again," Lake repeats the announcement. *"Everyone should be dressed and ready in ten minutes."*

No, she misheard Lake. Samara can't trust a damn thing—not her hearing, not her eyes. Last night she slept fully clothed in her bathtub with music playing loudly to drown out the night noises. She even wore sneakers in case she had to run out of her apartment. Thankfully, the apparitions didn't appear. No grunting sounds or beady glowing eyes staring back at her. No one pleading for help.

In the mirror, she practices her grin. This unrecognizable person is going to keep it together because she has no other choice.

Samara exits the restroom and approaches her office with trepidation. She braces herself for what tricks her mind will present her with. When she unlocks the door, she lets out a sigh of relief. There's still a slight smell of smoke in the air, but there's no Piedad. On a rack, Samara hangs a garment bag containing what she'll wear tonight.

The halter dress is stunning in a dark crimson color, and backless right down to the top of her ass. The front of the garment has intricate embroidered flowers with threads fragmenting to appear ripped and shredded. A leather choker covers the neck clasped together with a leather flower in the back. Tommy managed to leave a small imprint of his own talent with the choker while still incorporating Antonio's signature DNA into his design.

Antonio was very specific about what he wanted everyone to wear today. As Samara may be interviewed as the West Coast voice of the brand while he's in New York, Antonio wanted to make sure she wore something tied to his earlier designs. So he asked her to wear this version of The Ramona gown, slightly modernized with Tommy's help. Too bad Tommy won't get any of the credit tonight unless Antonio decides to toss him a bone.

Models are set to arrive around 3 P.M., with the show scheduled to start at 5 P.M. West Coast time, 8 P.M. East Coast time. Another designer's much bigger show will be running in New York at the same time as Antonio's Vernon show, but there wasn't much they could do about the schedule. Most of the reporters will be covering the New York show anyway. Samara will also run interference with the press with the help of the publicists, making sure any influencer–celebrity starlets get photographed.

She slips into the dress very easily. It sculpts her thin body perfectly. Samara feels sexy and at least she has that, a facade of strength made possible by this garment.

Samara tries to reach the hook on the choker but can't. Her fingers are slippery, an indication of just how fragile she feels—like she'll soon disintegrate into pieces.

"Can someone please help me with this?" she yells out. The more she struggles, the more she feels this simple thing is an omen of how she will inevitably fail. "Anyone!"

A person reaches from behind and gently presses on her shoulder. They hook the choker and make sure the garment flows correctly against her slender figure. Their touch is firm as they manipulate the bodice to detangle any loose threads. The familiarity of the way they move her body causes Samara to suddenly shudder.

Abuela Lola used to do this. The way her grandmother jostled her body about to pin a fabric tighter, or cinch it a bit here and there. Sometimes Abuela Lola would use her scissors and snip the material right off her frame. The gleam of the scissors used to scare and excite her. One wrong move and Samara would be cut—but that never happened. Her grandmother was always so careful yet confident in the way she worked.

What would her grandmother think of Samara now? Would she even recognize her? How upset would she be? Abuela Lola warned Samara about something before she died but Samara didn't listen. Couldn't listen. What was it Abuela Lola said? It's right there, at the very edge of her mind but Samara can't take hold of the memory. It slips away from her.

She turns around and comes face-to-face with Dolores. The seamstress has loosened the severity of her bun for once. Her gray hair cascades down to her back. She doesn't wear her usual dowdy uniform. Instead, Dolores is wearing a vibrant blue shift dress that highlights the hints of green in her light brown eyes, something Samara hasn't noticed before. It's true what Antonio said about her: Dolores is beautiful.

"Thank you," Samara says.

Dolores is not looking at her but past her. Samara is invisible, made of delicate chiffon.

"You're welcome," Dolores says, but her lips aren't moving.

Samara's not sure if she made that part up or if her eyes are deceiving her again. When the woman starts to walk away, she becomes desperate.

"Wait!" she shouts. "Dolores, will you be here tonight?"

Samara doesn't understand why she's asking this, but it feels important.

"Of course. I never miss a show." The seamstress still doesn't meet her eyes. She gazes beyond her, and that causes Samara to crave the attention more than anything, to be seen.

"I haven't had any more episodes," she says. "I feel so much better."

Dolores presses her lips together. She doesn't believe her, but Samara keeps talking.

"My grandmother warned me about being too sensitive. She said I felt everything too deeply and that's what made me a good writer. I never thought that was true, but maybe she was right."

This isn't the warning Abuela Lola gave Samara before she died. It's just another crumb she offers; anything to make Dolores stay. She waits for the seamstress to say something, but she doesn't. Dolores just stands there staring past her.

"Anyway, I just wanted to thank you for not telling anyone about what happened," she says. "I'm fine now."

The seamstress nods her head, then finally looks squarely at Samara.

"Estamos aquí a la orden."

Samara tears up immediately. It's something Abuela Lola would always say to the clients after finishing up their order. *Estamos aquí a la orden.* We are here to serve you.

Dolores walks away and Samara tries not to feel gutted by this minor interaction. The leather choker squeezes her neck. It's so hard to swallow, but once she takes a shot, she manages to conceal her sorrow again like she's been doing ever since she moved to Vernon.

CHAPTER 33

GUESTS GATHER IN front of the building under oversized umbrellas held open by interns. They're annoyed at having to wait, but wait they will, since the show won't be ready for at least another hour. The rain is just a drizzle, but it's enough to grate on everyone's nerves. The steady shower adds a dampness to the air, a heaviness. The crowd is lucky. The Vernon perfume has decided to give them a reprieve, but who knows when they might be coated with the stench.

As the sedans with tinted windows pull up in front to deposit the VIPs, Samara makes sure the guests are quickly escorted in and made to pose in front of the step-and-repeat banner. It's hard to figure out which reality show wannabe is important to Antonio or to the brand, but Samara helps make the call.

"So happy you made it," she says to a teen TV star. The actress is in head-to-toe Mota, the outfit messengered to her that very morning, payment already made guaranteeing her appearance tonight. Samara directs the photographer to take her photo and sits the celebrity beside a reporter.

"Get that idiot out of there. He's nobody and is going to mess up the op," someone yells into the headset Samara is forced to wear. The audio contraption is a constant chorus of different voices barking out orders. It's all so dizzying to follow and just adds to her anxiety.

"This isn't your seat," Samara says to a beautiful young man in a vibrant, floral suit, clearly vintage, but not Mota. "We have you over here."

The man gets up without making a fuss and follows Samara to another seat that will block most of his view.

When she can, Samara allows interesting attendees who have a compelling aesthetic to come out of the rain, but only if they're wearing the designer. They're who Antonio should be creating for: L.A. innovators who are bold and don't give a fuck about New York or Paris. They embody the Antonio Mota from before. Samara even loves the way they sit in the front row, so full of arrogance.

Photographers position themselves in a tight fit at the end of the runway, jostling for the best spot. The area is so claustrophobic, like they're trapped in a pen wielding their bulky cameras as weapons.

"Brandon is here," Lake says as Samara heads back outside to see who else she can wrangle from the crowd. She stops and searches for the familiar white beard, but finds none. Brandon has shaved his face clean. It's all pink and glistening. Without facial hair, he looks younger, his boyish mischievousness even more visible than before.

"You're gorgeous," he says.

"Who told you this was a good idea?" She playfully slaps his face.

"What? You don't like it?" He rubs his chin. "My barber convinced me it was time to let go. Now you get to see the real me."

Lisa runs up to her and tells her something about a missing model. Before tending to that mess, Samara ushers Brandon to his seat.

"Anything I can do to help?" he asks.

"Not unless you can strike a pose," she says. "I can't wait to be on the other side of this."

"Soon it will be over," he says. "And all that will be left will be your beauty."

"Shut up." She leaves him with the friends she met at the dinner. They're not in the front row but close enough, eagerly staring at the mouth of the runway.

The set is not as intricate a battle scene as planned, but it is still impressive. The battle symbolizes how the industry wanted to throw Antonio away, and how he fought to get to where he is now.

Everything has been timed to the second. As soon as the last model leaves the runway, a spotlight will shine to reveal the virtual image of the giant "Ramona" rising up again from the ashes of war. The virtual model will be beaming in from New York in a glorious red gown. The Vernon show will end and cut to the pumping sound of the runway show in New York, reflecting the dawn of a new day. Or it's what they hope will happen. The storm looming over the California sky is causing some technical difficulties.

We see you! You look beautiful!

Samara hearts texts from her family and friends tuning in to the livestream. Someone promised to help set up her parents with the video. She hasn't bothered checking in with them in weeks. They have no idea what's been going on with her. No one does. But at least she looks good.

Backstage, Samara finds a corner to swallow a couple of pills with the help of a glass of champagne. The pills will wake her up and slow down the alcohol. Her tongue licks the edges of her teeth. They feel like glass that will break from how much she's been clenching her jaw.

Last-minute adjustments are being made to the models as they line up, waiting for their cue to begin their walk. The models teeter around like giant gazelles wrapped up in leather and flowing chiffon. The focal point of their makeup is a black, smokey eye with a nude lip. Some of them hoist up rifle-purses. They aim at one another pretending to shoot. The backstage photographers eat it up.

The air is electric. Everyone is so amped, so ready, even Samara can't help herself. She touches the models to make sure they're real. This is all real.

"What is the hold-up?"

Antonio yells for the show to begin on time. His voice is being broadcast into everyone's headset, including Samara's, and she prays someone else will answer the irate designer.

"On hold for one more guest," someone calmly says.

Samara hunts through the crowd until she sees Lake gesturing for her. In front of Lake is Olivia Celis, wearing a gown with an exaggerated bustle in neon green. The matriarch takes small steps and Samara rushes to help her by gently taking her by the arm.

"Are you comfortable?" Samara asks when she seats her in the front row, but when she looks at Olivia, her face has turned green—a look of death.

Disturbed by what she sees, Samara runs backstage and takes cover behind Tommy.

"It's almost time!" Tommy grabs her by the waist and lifts her up for a spin. The models laugh, but they sound like squealing pigs being led to slaughter. Their eyes are black coals.

"Oh my god," Samara says. "Please stop."

But that makes everyone laugh even harder.

"This is going to be great! This is going to be great! This is going to . . ."

Samara winces. She's not inebriated enough for this and she has to remedy that, but the lights go down.

It begins.

CHAPTER 34

THE FIRST MODEL struts down the runway like a show horse. She wears a floor-length dress with an exaggerated dome shape reminiscent of turn-of-the-century skirt bustles. The high collar conceals her long neck, but the bodice opens into a keyhole that accentuates her chest. A sumptuous silk, the flowing fabric glides behind her like smoke. This is an untainted Ramona, an innocent. The first before all others. She displays a sly smirk, flashing just a hint of wickedness before turning back up the runway.

The show's producer nudges the next model out, and then the next. In everyone's headset, Antonio barks out orders or insults. Sometimes the words make no sense, just gibberish entering Samara's head adding to the soundtrack of absurdity.

"Why can't she walk faster!" he screams.

When Samara turns to watch, the model speeds across the runway like a button was pressed to make her accelerate. Her stomps sound like firecrackers going off. Samara begins to laugh uncontrollably but when she seeks out Tommy for validation, he just stares at her with dead eyes.

"No laughing," she scolds herself, fixing her face. "This is serious business."

When she goes back to observing the runway, this time the model is walking excruciatingly slow. Samara's mind is fucking with her. She squeezes her eyes shut for a few seconds, but the model's movement continues to be snaillike.

"What is wrong with her?" she asks. "Why is she doing that?"

The model has beautiful indigenous features that contrast against her straight, white-blonde hair. Her mouth is parted and the rigid edges of her teeth shimmer. One tooth is covered by a gold cap with a small Antonio Mota logo on it. Samara stares in horror at the pinkness of the model's moist tongue, licking her mouth before biting a piece of her bottom lip clean off.

Each model does something disturbing, but only Samara can see it. No one else seems to notice a thing. They're too busy screaming for the next model to go or appeasing Antonio in their headset as he gives them notes in real time. The audience watches the show with their phones in front of their faces—except for Olivia. The matriarch simply sits there with her hands neatly placed atop her lap. Olivia's composure feels so otherworldly, so rooted in the past. Perhaps it's the way she's dressed that makes Samara think this, or the way she's so rigid in her posture, like a dueña—the owner of everything.

When Samara shifts her head away for a second, the present moment adjusts itself again. Both the music and the models are back in tune to the same rhythm. As the models arrive backstage, they change into another outfit. Dolores and the seamstresses are at the ready to hide any mistakes in the clothes. Tommy is also running around making sure everything is perfect and to Antonio's liking.

The lights are lowered again to mark the beginning of another chapter in Antonio's storied design life. The progression of The Ramona is spotlighted with words projected against a wall:

Animus

Resist

Antonio had approved select phrases or words from Samara's writings to use. That morning he was still making changes to the choices. The word selections all center on the Battle of La Mesa. The last armed resistance during the Mexican-American War was held on these very streets, solidifying the city of Vernon as property of the United States. The same words are also being projected against a building in New York.

Resist

The words travel across the runway and are now projected onto the audience. The projection suddenly stops on the face of one person, then slowly moves to another, then another. Audience members become sitting targets—wearing what Samara wrote.

A short pause and the change in the soundtrack marks a new batch of designs. This time the clothes are more rugged; less refined, only united in the theme of how the wearer battles each day by putting on armor. The body is restricted in leather and distressed denim as if the models had constructed the clothes themselves with found scraps.

A model holds the rifle purse across her shoulders, resting it against the back of her neck like a barbell. When she reaches the end of the runway, she "shoots" at the photographers. The music is perfectly timed so that the drums sound like gunshots. Each "shot" causes Samara to jump.

"Oh my god," she says. Her nerves can't take it, so she searches backstage for a drink. Not paying attention, she trips over some shoes but Lake is there to pick her up.

"It's too much," she says, half-serious, half-joking.

"Here, take this. This will calm you down." Lake pulls a tiny gold case from her pocket and offers her a pill. Without even asking what it is, Samara puts it in her mouth. Samara is willing to ingest whatever will lead her down the rabbit hole.

"Can I have one?" Rosa appears out of nowhere.

The three of them press their heads together so no one else can see what they're doing. They're like the witches in that Shakespeare play, brewing ugly spells with toxic concoctions.

"Rosa," Dolores calls from across the way. Just one word from the seamstress and the trio feels caught in the act. But Dolores is not family or blood; she's just Samara's co-worker, a religious old woman who wants to put a stop to a good time. Samara has already forgotten their earlier interaction. There is no room for the past. The three ignore her.

When Rosa rejoins the other seamstresses, Dolores swiftly reprimands her in a harsh whisper. Samara's eyes stay glued to the quiet but dramatic interaction. Dolores's expression transforms into disappointment, then anger, but Rosa retorts and storms off.

"Someone is putting on their big-girl pants," Lake says.

"If one of us falls," Samara says, "we all fall."

She doesn't want to be the only one feeling this strange misery. She wants Rosa and Lake and the interns and everyone backstage to fall into the pit with her. After all, there could be nothing wrong if everyone is engaged in the same demonic dance.

Tommy fixes the black veil covering the final model's face. The Ramona dress is worn again, only this time it has become a war-torn wedding gown. The remake is shredded with cutouts across the chest and back. She is the survivor of this war, the last woman standing. Dark, almost black lipstick covers her full lips and diamond teardrops fall down her cheeks.

When Samara looks at the model's hands, she swears they're covered in blood, but it is the trick of a garish red strobe light bouncing to the music.

"Go, go, go!"

At the end of the runway, a hologram appears to connect this show to the one about to begin in New York. The hologram showcases the new Ramona, a modern warrior dressed in a long silk gown that cascades against her lithe silhouette. Just as before, the hologram towers over everything, a giant ready to swallow them whole.

The model reaches out to touch the bridal Ramona. They pretend to hold hands, but the hologram is frozen, stuck in its disconnected message. The audience isn't aware of the mistake, but everyone in New York is. They scream their dismay into the headsets. Samara yanks it off her head.

But the mistake makes sense to her, the way the monstrous model glitches grotesquely. Whatever pill Samara took makes her body feel like liquid. Beads of sweat gather on the back of her neck. She's melting.

"How do you feel?" Lake asks.

"I feel nice," Samara says. "Like nothing can hurt me."

As for Antonio's team backstage, they gather around computer screens and phones, waiting with bated breath for the other runway show to start. Antonio can't blame them for the timing being off on their end. They did what they had to do. Now it's on New York to continue the story they started in Vernon and bring it to its grand finale.

CHAPTER 35

THE NEW YORK show begins with the poet Excelia reciting her ephemeral reflections on the future. Unlike Samara's, the poet's words were not edited down or put through hundreds of revisions. Excelia submitted her poetry a week ago and Antonio said he loved it, even though he didn't. A trio of string musicians accompany the poet, playing a haunting melody. When the writer reaches the end of her recitation, the model depicted by the hologram just seconds ago in Vernon struts down the runway.

Antonio's Vernon team holds one another while watching all their hard work go up and down the runway. The audience also follows along to the New York show, which is being projected on a wall.

It's obvious to everyone that the models in New York are better in every way: They have stronger walks, they have bigger names, they're skinnier. They stand out because money was spent to make sure they would. Samara watches intently, waiting for something strange to happen, but there are no technical issues and nothing out of the ordinary that only she can see. This allows her to be present to what the designer has been creating these past few months.

Antonio's sartorial vision of the future is both sensual and ecstatic, a celebration of female survival. His Ramona has thrived after the "war," her regalia a seductive combination of leather and silk, soft and hard. Each design a defiant existence of beauty. *This* is why Samara wanted to work with Antonio: to be a witness to his brilliance.

And just like that, the runway show is over. Everyone, including the audiences on both coasts, claps and cheers. Even tears are shed, but not by Samara. All she feels is a sense of release. The whole ordeal is over, and she's managed to survive it.

"We did it! We killed it." Tommy grabs her and kisses her on the lips. "They murdered it! Blood on the floor! Blood on the floor!"

"But is Antonio happy with the way it all went down?"

"Antonio? Who fucking cares! We're about to forget him and everything we went through to get to this day."

The audience quickly exits, unable to avoid the downpour that's drenching the city. A select few stay behind. Jonathan pops open a champagne bottle and glasses are filled. Reporters line up to interview Tommy to get his take on the show. He's rehearsed his approved quotes, but he's also smart enough to subtly point out which designs were his. Alex takes over DJ duties and connects the music to the building's intercom system. Soon, everyone is dancing to a playlist of rap and house music.

The floors become slick and wet from spilt drinks. On the slippery surface, Samara spins and spins. A strobe light flickers on and off, brightening even the dark corners. She loses herself in the music.

Alex grabs Samara and starts to grind into her. She pulls out her phone and makes Samara take a photo. When Alex shows Samara the picture, their heads are decapitated, bleeding from the neck, like the women in Marisa Sol's paintings.

"Do you see that?" Samara screams.

"We're beautiful," Alex says. "Fucking beautiful."

Samara doesn't question her. Instead, she follows her to the bathroom to sniff coke like it's the eighties. The music gets harder to follow. Her legs are moving, but she doesn't know how it's possible. As in the photograph, she feels like her head is no longer part of her body.

The room whirls out of control and Samara can barely catch her breath. She pushes against those around her to land in a corner where she tries to regroup. But the room slowly tilts upside down.

"There you are."

Brandon covers her lips with his.

"I need this all to stop," she says. "Just for a little while."

He grabs her and they run through the crowd, her heart pounding. He squeezes her ass and when they kiss again, she can taste hard liquor and citrusy lime.

"Come on," she says.

The door to the Library is open and Samara pulls him in without thinking of how much the room scares her. She's fully succumbing to the madness, allowing the numbness that has been growing inside of her since she boarded the flight to California to fully take over. The stress of all her hard work has ended and she's about to let herself be undone.

Brandon and Samara don't bother turning on the lights. They fuck standing against the table. He flips her around and Samara clutches at its edges.

When he's done—and he's done quickly—Brandon zips up

his pants. Samara's dress has a tear in the hem. She pokes a finger through it, making the hole worse.

"We should get back out there," he says. "Don't want anyone to miss us, do you?"

"What are you talking about?" She pulls down her skirt. "Are you crazy? Who cares?"

"I'm sorry. I have to take care of some business. It's dumb but it won't take long. I promise."

"Yeah, fine. Whatever." She doesn't sound annoyed, but she is. He's behaving like a fuckboi because he's always been one, and does any of it really matter? Brandon's just part of the mayhem, the disorder of her life.

"I'm about to burn what's left of my brain cells," Samara says. "By the time you see me again, I will have entered a whole other plane of existence."

"I promise to check in with you later. The night, it's just starting." He tries to kiss her one more time but Samara pushes him away. He leaves wearing his usual naughty expression, a Latino Cheshire Cat.

Samara flicks the light switch on and stands in front of the mirror. Her lipstick is smeared across her face. She finds a box of tissues and reapplies. Her movements are lethargic and labored like the models moving in slow motion. She's so wasted.

When her eyes shift back to the table, Samara sees a familiar item that wasn't there before. She knows exactly what it is. She's so afraid.

Samara's fingers hover over the photo. Piedad peeks from behind the curtain like she always has, no evidence that the photo had ever been engulfed in flames. She picks it up and the Piedad in the snapshot starts to cry in a silent pantomime. Samara drops the photo, horrified.

"I can't," she cries. "I can't take this anymore."

The grunting begins and Samara rushes to the door, but it is locked. She pounds at it with her fists but no one hears her, not with the loud music playing. Everyone is having a good time while she screams in terror, trapped inside the Library.

"Open the fucking door!"

A tapping of hooves against the concrete floor emerges from somewhere inside. She screams for help until her voice goes hoarse.

She hears footsteps behind her. Heels against the floor. One step. Then another. Samara slowly turns.

Piedad.

Piedad is here. She wears the exact same clothing as in the picture. But her lips are not sewn together and there are no maggots falling from her, no blood dripping. She seems so real, so human. Samara's whole body convulses.

The apparition steps closer, until her icy cheek is pressed against Samara's—the touch of death upon her.

"Te diré un cuento," Piedad says.

CHAPTER 36

"I DON'T WANT TO KNOW," Samara pleads. Her trembling knees knock against each other. "Please, I don't want to know."

"Close your eyes," Piedad says in her heavily accented English.

This will be Samara's end, right here, in Antonio's archives. They'll find her here like they did the other day, but this time she'll be dead. Samara weeps.

"Primero, empezamos con una canción."

"La zorrita, zorrita, señores, se fue a la cañada . . ."

Somewhere a voice sings a lively tune that clashes against the terror eating away at Samara's being. She doesn't want to die. Not here, not now. She's too fucking young. Too fucking smart to let this happen to her.

"No!" Samara pulls away and runs to the door. It suddenly flings open and she falls. When she gets up, she's no longer at the party. There's no Alex grinding on someone. No Brandon. The tiled floor is gone, replaced with dirt, and everything is different. Samara's view is of an open space, like she's outside.

Simple facades of wooden structures line what should be the walls. Leaves from the trees dotting the area cover the ground. The Saprophyte is unrecognizable. She races toward the main entrance to get away but can't find it. When she turns to try another path, Samara is frozen by what she sees.

A teen sells strawberries. She holds a wooden crate close to her chest. Samara recognizes her immediately as a younger Piedad. A group of men slow down their gait to catch a glimpse of the Latina beauty. These courteous men take off their hats and place them across their chests. The innocent Piedad offers her smile freely.

The men look every bit as real as Samara is. Sweat trickles down their foreheads. One of them smokes and Samara can smell the tobacco. When the men buy fruits from Piedad, they then turn to Samara and offer her a strawberry. They look her up and down, licking their lips and saying vulgar piropos to her—how she is as juicy as the strawberry and how they can't wait to taste her. Samara screams and runs in the opposite direction.

When she reaches the Finance wing of the building, Samara comes across women in prayer inside a conference room. The table has been replaced with wooden pews and a cross. The women in the congregation hold hands and sway. A slightly older Piedad follows along, but her eyes glance back to where Samara stands. Suddenly, the women tear at their clothes, screeching their agony in tongues . . . but not Piedad, who only stares at Samara.

Before she can comprehend any of this, Samara stumbles out of there and finds herself in Seamstress Row. The sewing machines are gone. Piedad works on a dress by hand. She's surrounded by Latinas who care for her, who warn her not to fall into traps. They tease her and offer her advice, and Piedad listens, but then a beautiful man appears and catches her eye. He gives her a sprig of lavender.

Piedad steals one of the dresses she helped make. She admires herself in the full-length mirror. The chiffon fabric flows to the ground in a vibrant red. With her hair secured up in a loose bun, the leather flower accent on the dress can be seen gracing her slender neck. The last items she takes are white opera gloves. Piedad strolls to Samara and stops in front of her, displaying a sheepish grin. It's the look of a person who is not used to doing anything bad, but for once is trying on a wicked persona.

Samara watches Piedad leave Seamstress Row to meet the man. They enter Antonio's office, which is now a saloon. So many people are crowded in there, laughing and singing along to a woman playing the guitar. Piedad is offered a drink.

Samara groans when the man is rough with Piedad, but she doesn't look away from the brutality. She feels it, each punch, each disgusting thrust. His hands on Piedad's throat are also on her throat, and she can't breathe.

"No! Please, no!" she cries. Flashes of Piedad's past play before her like a waking dream and she's the sole audience. "No more."

She races down a hallway, trying to get away from such violence. She runs to the cafeteria, hoping to find a place to hide. Instead, she finds the men from the framed photos on the wall, now made flesh. They pull down their suspenders. On the cafeteria table lies a barely conscious Piedad. She's being held down while the men joke amongst themselves. Piedad's mouth is covered with a handkerchief. Her eyes go wild.

"Come back here, little pig!"

One of the men yells at Samara to join them and she backs out of there in shock. The men shout for her to return, to not be afraid. Their maniacal laughter howls across the hallways. "Little piggy! Little piggy!"

Now Samara runs past boxers fighting each other in a boxing ring. Blood stains their chests. She slips on a pool of blood trying to get away. There are hordes of workers, women and men, in their uniforms huddled together in a corner, on their break. They eat strawberries, their mouths red with the fruity pulp. The workers become ill. They bend over in pain, clutching their stomachs and throwing up.

She tries to locate the exit that leads to the parking lot, but there are no doors. There is no way out. Soon the pigs come. A large drove of pigs barrel down a hallway, snorting and bumping against the walls. Their hooves trample Piedad's body, which is now lying on the floor, perfectly still. There are so many. The animals have done this before, to other women, other girls, those who do not cooperate. The pigs get them all in the end.

Piedad never screams, not once. She only grunts.

Soon the pigs turn their focus to Samara. They barrel toward her, snorting heavily, guts dripping from their snouts.

"Help me! Help me!"

Samara shrieks and runs until she hits a wall, trying to get away from the animals. Her nails tear into Antonio's wallpaper until her fingers bleed trying to find purchase on the bathroom door, but it's no use. The building no longer exists, not the way it used to be. The only thing that does is this history of pain. There's no escaping it. Piedad is the messenger, and Samara must witness it all and suffer.

She screams in horror, still digging into the walls while the pigs draw nearer.

CHAPTER 37

But the pigs never reach her. They suddenly vanish, as do the boxers and the seamstresses, the evil men and the thrashing parishioners. They disappear, and all that is left is Samara in hysterics. She crumbles to the floor.

"La zorrita, zorrita, señores . . ."

It takes a long time, but eventually Samara gets up. The door to the Library is still open. The sounds of the pigs and the men no longer exist. There's only that sweet voice singing. She follows the song back to where the archives are stored.

She enters and the door closes behind her. Her whole being is sorrow. Samara touches her throat and is reminded of her night with Brandon, but not just that night. She recalls dark secrets she's been unable to shake off no matter how much she tries to drink the memories away. The job at Vernon came right when she needed to bury them. Everyone could argue it was the death of Abuela Lola that made her take the job and move across the country, but that wasn't the complete truth. It was just a part of the story.

It's amazing how Piedad has chosen her to be the witness to these disturbing truths. Samara understands the reason behind it now, even if she wishes Piedad hadn't picked her. There are moments in a person's life when choice is taken away, when those in power believe in bending reality to their will. Piedad is reliving the horror of her death in a disturbing spiral and craving to be heard. All the while, Samara has been unable to face the truth of her own personal terror.

These women across time and generations have shared the same agony. Piedad, Abuela Lola, and Samara, a trio of women who have each been preyed upon by pigs.

There was a story Samara uncovered in her research that she didn't include in the beautiful feature she wrote that set her on this path to Vernon. She didn't want to taint her grandmother's history, although she knew the truth. Abuela Lola always said the city made her, but also that it almost broke her.

"Most people are wolves and they see us only as prey. Not all people—not your grandfather or the neighbors who surrounded me," Abuela Lola said. "But there are wolves out there dressed in beautiful clothes, and they mean to trick you. If you don't pay attention, if you let your guard down, they'll devour you."

Abuela Lola spoke of treacherous men who took advantage of young girls. She talked about evil women who helped these men, but she also talked about the importance of surrounding yourself with trustworthy people.

"The women who worked together side by side in the factory would always tell you who to avoid and who to not spend time alone with," she said. "They'd remind you it's important to not be lured by shiny, bright things."

The one thing Samara was always certain about throughout childhood was that she was Abuela Lola's favorite. Abuela Lola loved her like no one else did. She pushed her to write her feelings down, reminded her that she had a gift and to not squander it.

She can sense that her grandmother is right there in the Library, delivering her warnings once again. The guilt she feels is so unbearable and has been weighing down on her for so long. The lie Samara constructed around her was made of the flimsiest of materials and she could only certify it by drinking.

Abuela Lola had told her to stop. She said she could see Samara's future and how it could all go down the drain, but Samara didn't want to hear it.

Even during those final days, when everyone seemed certain her grandmother would not last the week, Samara buried herself with "work" and alcohol. It was easy to just check out from the family drama when everyone around her was so attuned to preparing for Abuela Lola's journey to the other side. They couldn't count on her. Her mother was so angry at having to bear the burden of her own mother's death by herself.

One night, Samara barely managed to pull herself together enough to give her mother a reprieve from watching over Abuela Lola. She sat by the sickbed and stared at her grandmother's chest rising and falling. When her grandmother had difficulty breathing, Samara would take a sip from her tumbler, which was filled mostly with vodka, before helping to adjust her pillows.

"He thought I was going to take the place of his wife, but I said no," Abuela Lola said, talking to her like a friend and not like she was her granddaughter. Seeing her so distraught frightened Samara. She wasn't sure what to do.

"Who?" she asked.

"Tío Francisco loved his rum so much. All day long he

drank," Abuela Lola said. "He took hold of me. He said I owed him. Didn't he send for me? Didn't he give me a new life in California?"

Abuela Lola started to cry, and Samara didn't know how to console her, not when she wanted to dive inside her drink and drown.

"Tío Francisco forced me to do it, but I didn't want to," Abuela Lola said, sobbing. "I wasn't the only one. He did it to others, but no one would believe me. Why would they? Everyone loved him."

Abuela Lola grabbed Samara's wrist hard enough to make her cower from the pain. She yanked Samara toward her on the bed. Her grandmother's breath smelled sour. Samara didn't want to be so close, to see death hovering right beside her.

"Stay away from his son, Benjy. When I die, he won't be afraid to show his face at the funeral, but don't let him fool you. He's the devil like his father," she said. "You don't remember, do you? Pobrecita. Mi Samara. It's best you forget."

She didn't want to let go, but Samara pried her fingers off.

Abuela Lola died the next day.

In a blur of alcohol, Samara attended the funeral. When Benjamin approached her, Samara's whole body went rigid like marble. It was immediate, the sensation of powerlessness in the face of something so wrong and evil.

"You've grown so much," he said, but his smile was a wicked mask. The memory of him standing over her as a child flooded her mind, a monstrous image she'd blocked for so many years. But the smell of his potent cologne sent her reeling back in time. What he did to her that night came over her like a tidal wave.

"Get the fuck away from me!" she lashed out.

Everyone thought it was just the drink talking. Soon after, Samara left for Vernon.

"I was so young," Samara says to Piedad, who suddenly appears. She stands there in the archives, stoic like a statue. "I still don't remember all of it. Just certain things. Fragments. An obscene touch. The stench of his cologne."

The moment is perfect for ugly secrets to be revealed.

"Abuela Lola was dying and I didn't want to see her that way, to have that memory of her imprinted in my mind, so I drank. But the truth was I just didn't want to think of how my grandmother was raped by her uncle and how his son did the same to me."

Maybe death is still waiting for her, but at least Samara, by confessing her secret, is absolved a tiny bit from what's been eating her alive all these months. Not just the horrible visions and fear, but the weight of shame, of not having control, of being consumed by monsters. Does it run in the family, this curse? Maybe that was why Samara's been drinking. She's been using alcohol to erase a family's hideous history.

Piedad and Samara examine each other. Piedad is so beautiful, but there's also a quiet rage behind those eyes. Samara recognizes it. It's the same anger Abuela Lola had throughout her life, that she used as a shield to protect her loved ones and herself.

It's close to two in the morning. Piedad leaves the archives and Samara follows behind her. The party has long ended but there are remnants of it visible everywhere, from empty bottles to food thrown on the floor. As a joke, someone left a freeze-framed video of Antonio on the wall. His giant face is stuck in a grimace, disapproving the partiers on their last stand.

Samara follows Piedad to the back of the factory. She leads her toward the Shipping and Receiving Department. The ever-present song is now replaced with the sound of people talking and clinking bottles. All the workers had been told to leave early to make room for the show. Piles of boxes are ready to be shipped the next day and they create a perfect fort to conceal Samara.

Just past the boxes, a group of men circle around a woman. Their backs are to Samara and a solitary light illuminates their cruel intentions.

"Don't."

A disheveled Rosa barely stands. Her legs are wobbly, but the men keep her propped up. They press a drink to her mouth.

"Just drink this," someone says. "This is better than water."

"She better be flexible," another voice adds. Their laughter bounces off the walls and echoes across the cavernous space.

"No," Rosa mumbles.

"Shhh. It's not going to take long," another woman's voice joins the men, cooing like a dove. Samara recognizes it immediately.

"You said you wanted to branch out. To do something more than just work as a seamstress," Lake says. She lightly taps Rosa's cheeks to revive her. "You're so pretty. You really are. Now open your mouth."

CHAPTER 38

These men can't wait to see who will be the first to pull it out. The wolves are right here, gnashing their teeth and salivating.

"We can get her to Vegas tonight. She'll be ready to go," another voice says. They're talking like they're ordering room service. The men taunt Rosa while plying her with more drinks.

The loop is not with Piedad reliving her trauma and sharing it with Samara. The loop is in how history repeats itself. Samara can't hide behind the allure of being accepted by those in power, not when others are paying the price. She searches for Piedad for guidance, but she's gone.

Samara is alone.

A guy, Samara remembers his name as Brian, places his hand atop Rosa's head. He pushes her down to her knees.

No no no.

Samara steps into view.

"What the fuck are you doing?" she yells. "Get the fuck away from her!"

For once her voice is strong and guttural. Not the white voice she's been employing at work for months but her Jersey voice, the one she uses with her friends. The one her family is used to. Her real voice.

The men staring back at her are the ones she met before at Olivia's private dinner. Tech bros with money and a lot to say about the future of Vernon. Someone gives a nervous laugh, which adds to the nightmarish atmosphere.

"Samara, what are you doing here? Everyone left to get drinks." Lake immediately tries to take control of the situation. "This is not a big deal."

"Get away her from her."

The guys look guilty. They raise their hands as if Samara is aiming a gun, but it's all for show. They're drunk, swaying to a silent beat.

"Rosa just wanted to have a good time." Lake is the only one talking. Her voice is brittle. "Samara, it's not what you think."

Of everyone there, Lake is the most sober and composed of the bunch. Now Samara can see it: She wants to be in charge so badly.

"Lake, this is not cool," one of the guys complains. "We were just having fun."

Samara kneels by Rosa, who has slumped to the floor, mumbling to herself incoherently. She calls for her mom and she's a little girl again, wanting to wake up from a bad dream. Samara uses the hem of her dress to dry Rosa's tears.

"Rosa, it's me. It's Samara. It's over now," she says. "They're not going to hurt you anymore. I promise."

"I didn't want to do it," Rosa cries out. She covers her face in shame. "I said no."

"It's okay," Samara says. "I'm going to get us help."

The men are reluctant to leave, but they eventually do. They pick up bottles from the floor and finish them. The plan is to just hop on a private jet to Vegas, to continue the party as planned.

Lake follows the men out, begging them to reconsider. She keeps insisting this is all a big misunderstanding, that she'll take care of it.

Cars rev up. Music from their stereo speakers cranks a hard bass. Soon they're gone.

"I'm so sorry, Rosa," Samara says. She looks for a cell phone to use but Rosa has nothing with her, not even her wallet. "Can you get up? I need to find help."

As much as she doesn't want to, Samara must leave her to call an ambulance and the cops.

Lake returns to them, clucking her tongue like a chicken. The song is being sung again, but Lake can't hear it. Somewhere nearby, Piedad is paying close attention.

"Samara, this is just a misunderstanding." Lake uses her receptionist voice on her, the one she deploys when dealing with irate customers. With every word she utters Samara notices how her voice becomes shriller, until it doesn't sound human at all. From the corner of her eye, Samara can see Lake's face morphing into a bird with a large beak and tiny beady eyes. She flutters her arms to get Samara's attention, flapping wings. Samara is too afraid to look directly at her.

"Rosa asked for this," Lake the bird says. The squawk of her voice grates on Samara like nails on a chalkboard. "So did you."

Rosa moans in front of her while this strange animal draws nearer. The hallucination continues to plague Samara but still, she must do something.

"Are you listening to me?" Lake screeches.

When Lake the bird grabs Samara, she stands and throws a sloppy punch right to the side of the bird's face. Lake falls back and hits her head hard on the cement floor.

Samara rubs her fist in pain and Lake's no longer a bird, just an ordinary, horrible woman.

"Jesus Christ, Samara. Calm down."

Brandon appears from behind a row of boxes. Samara's knees buckle. She should have expected this, for him to not only be here with his friends but to be the ringleader of this shit show. But in the back of her mind, she had hoped differently. That this had all been masterminded by Lake. That he wasn't part of this and that she wasn't wrong about him.

His face is red and sweaty. Now that he's beardless, she can see how round and piggish his nose is. He approaches her with a look of concern, feigning shock at the turn of events.

Suddenly, the first night they fucked comes back to Samara in clear flashes. Samara did want it, did ask for it—but not for everything they did that night. There were so many signs alerting her of exactly the type of man Brandon is. It wasn't just Piedad, but others who were also hinting at the truth. Dolores and the seamstresses tried to warn her. Marisa Sol. The pigs were right there, circling around Rosa and Samara. She was too consumed with succeeding at this job, with proving to her family back in Jersey that she could handle it all, at the cost of her health and her sanity. At the cost of her life.

"I always knew you were wild. I knew it the first time we met," he says, circling closer. "There's no reason to take it all out on poor Lake. The girl was just doing what we asked her to do. Taking initiative."

"Stay away from me," Samara says. She takes a step back, leaving Rosa on the floor between them. "Just get away from us."

Brandon shakes his head in disappointment.

"It's funny," he says. "I was just talking to Antonio, telling him how great the show was. We even talked about you. He really likes you."

Brandon blocks her way out. She needs to get away from him but running won't work, so she lets him keep talking while she searches for another exit.

"I need to help Rosa. Please, just leave us alone."

"No, no. What are you talking about? You're nothing like Rosa," he says. "Even my grandmother thinks you're special, not like the quiet sheep that follow her around, waiting for a handout. You're not like the others."

"Let me go get help for Rosa, Brandon."

"Are you going to punch me too?" He chuckles. "Look, I promise I won't do anything to you. Go ahead. Go help your tiny friend here. I swear I won't stop you."

It's a trap, but she has no other choice. So Samara makes a run for it, and Brandon almost allows her to pass, but then he yanks her by her hair and shoves her against a wall. Her chin hits the surface hard and rattles her brain. He turns her around to face him.

"Who do you think you are?"

His breath is hot and sticky. He nuzzles into her neck and gropes her.

"You really think you're better than this nothing on the floor?"

Samara doesn't say anything. Her mind detaches from her body and she can watch from above. He's turned on by this. She can feel his growing bulge against her groin.

"No, I'm nothing," she says, grimacing as he tries to find an opening to her dress. "I'm nothing, Brandon."

Instead of fighting back, she caresses his expensive suit. Brandon enjoys this act of submission. This is a different side of her, and he's pleased with this gentler Samara.

When she reaches down to unbuckle his pants, he nibbles on her neck and grunts in her ear like a pig. His nose is wet and cold. Samara wants to throw up. Across the way, Piedad appears, her face full of rage.

Samara strokes the front of his pants until Brandon loosens his grip.

"I knew you would understand," he says, moaning.

"Yes," she says. "I understand."

She grabs his groin so hard that if she could rip his dick off, she would. When he bends over in pain, she pushes him to the floor. Then she runs from Shipping and Receiving, back toward her office. When she makes it inside, she grabs Abuela Lola's scissors and runs.

CHAPTER 39

Samara holds the scissors in front of her and quietly crawls toward the main entrance. Somewhere in Shipping and Receiving, Brandon curses her name. When she opens the door, the noise alerts him and he soon chases after her.

"Help me! Please! He's trying to rape me!" Samara screams, but there's no one around. The rain is pouring down, making everything slick and slippery. The Vernon streets are as desolate as they always are. "Rape! Somebody! Rape!"

She runs and turns the corner.

"Let me explain!" Brandon yells. "This is just business. It has nothing to do with you. Stop running, Samara!"

Samara lands in front of the construction site. The Whole Foods sign flaps in the wind. But from within the structure, Samara finds Piedad peeking her head through the frame of what was once a window. She beckons her to come forward.

"Fuck," Samara says. "Fuck."

She gets to the wire fence, pulls it apart, and squeezes herself through the hole. The hem of her dress gets caught on a protruding nail.

"Samara, don't do this!" Brandon sounds so close. He stomps his way toward her.

She yanks her leg forward and screams when the wire cuts into her inner thigh. Samara sucks in the pain and limps toward the building with blood trickling down her leg. She climbs through the scaffolding and pushes the rusted door open.

When Brandon sees her, he picks up his pace.

Inside the empty building, Samara lumbers forward in complete darkness. There are broken tiles and glass everywhere, and huge gaps in the walls. Peeling paint drops from above. Samara curses at herself for not having a cell phone with her. The one time she's not stupidly documenting every fucking thing, the one time she needs it for real.

Someone is singing again, the same haunting song that has serenaded her for so many weeks. The tune echoes off the walls. It is eerie and not of this time, but definitely of this place. She follows the music.

Brandon calls out to her. His footsteps draw nearer. He is right in front of the building. She needs to keep moving. The song leads her to a room with long wooden tables, similar to Seamstress Row. There are no sewing machines but Samara imagines there must have been at one time.

Women's voices echo around her. She doesn't see them. They don't appear to her like Piedad, but she can hear them. They tease her. Some say how pretty she is. Others say she looks like a mess. They ask her what happened to her clothes and laugh.

"Ya viene. Do you hear him? He'll be here any minute, and then what?" they say. The women are eager for him to arrive. "Está por la puerta. Only a few more steps and he'll be here."

Samara waits for him to show up. This is what she's meant to do, and yet she's still so afraid.

"I just want to talk to you," Brandon calls out. "Stop overreacting!"

He enters the building and uses his cell phone flashlight to help find her.

A wind stirs past her. It feels like the women are going around in circles, like they're dancing. She can hear the sound of swooshing skirts and the *clip-clop* of heels against a wooden floor so clearly.

"Está aquî," the women say in unison. "Samara, despierta. He's right by the door."

Samara can't stop shaking. She moves to the center of the room.

The door creaks open.

"What the hell, Samara," Brandon says. "This is out of control, even for you."

She points the scissors at him.

"Seriously?" He shakes his head. "What are you going to do with those?"

When he enters the room, the women materialize behind him one by one, just like Piedad has done countless times. So many beautiful brown women of different ages—girls with long, stringy hair, women with blunt bob haircuts. Some are in modern clothes, factory uniforms, or simple cotton dresses. Others in late-Edwardian-era outfits just like the ones in the research that consumed Samara not too long ago. They cover their mouths to conceal their laughter, so as not to ruin the surprise.

Samara lowers the scissors and places them on a table. She knows now she won't need them.

"Listen, no one's getting hurt," he says. "Everyone gets paid. Even you, if you want to. Look at Lake. She's smart."

"And Rosa?" Samara asks. The timbre of her voice is even. After all, she's in on the surprise the women are planning for him, the evil joke about to be played. "She pays for it, doesn't she?"

"This is boring. Look at us. I'm all wet. You got me all dirty in this stupid place. For what?" he asks. "Let's just go back and clean ourselves up. Check on Rosa and make sure she's okay. Come on, Samara."

Brandon uses the charm he always uses to get what he wants. But no matter how sweetly he speaks, he can't conceal his anger. He has the same temper Samara noticed when she went to visit his grandmother. She remembers how Olivia's eyes blazed red when she asked about the Knitting Mills. It runs in the family, this indignation, this entitlement.

The women surround Brandon with disturbingly wide grins, the surprise about to reveal itself. They creep toward him until . . .

"What the fuck?" Brandon exclaims as he turns to face them.

A girl pushes him. Another pokes him from behind. Another pulls his hair. Another, his ear. They slap his cheeks. Curse his name, his family, his whole lineage.

Cochino. Perro. Rana. Mentiroso. Demonio. Diablo.

"Get off of me!" Brandon runs to the door to find it locked. There is real fear vibrating off his body. He tries to break free, but the ghosts of the women keep multiplying. More and more appear out of nowhere. He screams for help, but there's no one to stop this torment from finally ending. They push him to the ground.

"Samara, help me!"

Brandon reaches for her, a last-ditch effort to get out from under this deadly wave. His eyes dart about looking for an exit where there is none. The women hold Brandon's hands and legs down. There's a frenzy of unhinged joy. Laughing and cheering. Samara screams ecstatically along with them. The maddening crescendo escalates.

From a dark corner of the room, Piedad materializes. She picks up Abuela Lola's scissors and walks toward the center of the chaos. Everyone goes silent. Even Brandon stops fighting. Piedad is radiant and beautiful. Her hair is long, with loose waves framing her striking face. There's no makeup on her, just the slightest hint of rouge on her cheeks. She's powerful and ageless.

Piedad stands over the fallen Brandon, gripping the scissors. She lowers herself and straddles his body. Brandon squirms and Piedad leans in closer, wielding the scissors under his chin. Then she whispers in his ear and Brandon screams.

Before Piedad proceeds, she looks at Samara and nods. Samara runs out of the room. She tumbles out of the building, away from that place and from whatever is about to happen to Brandon.

CHAPTER 40

SHE LIMPS BACK. The rainstorm is now only a drizzle. Every step hurts, but it's not until Antonio Mota's building comes into view that she lets out a sob.

Trucks enter the city. It may be early Sunday morning, but the workweek is just about to begin. The taco truck is already setting up for breakfast. Across the street, groups of women and men disembark a city bus and head to Consuelo's Farmhouse to clock in at this ungodly hour for their weekend shift. They don't notice Samara, or if they do, they mind their business.

The security guard waves hello to her. Then he does a double take.

"Hey, everything okay?"

Samara just keeps walking, retracing her steps. Dawn will break soon and every horror this night produced is hopefully coming to an end.

Above the gates to the building is a plaque similar to the one found on the main entrance. Instead of it being a slick gold, the plaque is a simple wooden sign with the words "The Saprophyte" etched into it. It hangs from a nail.

Before Samara took the job, she had read all she could about Antonio. She made sure to commit to memory what the word *saprophyte* meant and why it was important to the designer. Antonio once said he wanted his creations to be parasitic, an organism that lives on forever, no matter what, even if it must survive off the essence of someone or something else.

"This shit," Samara says before yanking the sign off the wall and throwing it on the ground.

Inside, she detects movement in the Shipping and Receiving Department. Someone is with Rosa. Samara rushes even when the pain is too great.

The seamstresses, all dressed for church, surround Rosa and tend to her. A distraught Rosa cries into their arms. One of the seamstresses caresses her hair. Another holds her hand.

"Dolores?" Samara asks, stunned to see them.

Dolores stands within the circle holding a glass of water. She offers the glass to the seated Rosa, then uses a handkerchief to dry the young seamstress's tears.

When the seamstress notices Samara, she doesn't even seem to be surprised. Dolores walks over to her, takes off her shawl, and places it around Samara. The simple act of kindness is staggering. When Samara looks at her, she doesn't see Dolores. She sees her Abuela Lola. Abuela Lola in her bed, recounting her days in Vernon like she was reliving them once again. Her grandmother made a full life here in this city. She found and created a family that protected and saved her, carving a life of her own before setting up another in Jersey. Samara thought she was retracing her grandmother's steps, in a way, surpassing them. Instead, the seamstresses held a mirror for her to see her true self.

The seamstresses continue to tend to Rosa. One of them checks in on the ambulance and waits for it outside.

"Where is Lake?" Samara asks, finally noticing who is missing.

"She wasn't here when we arrived," Dolores says.

Where did that bitch go? Samara wonders. *Does she think the Celis family will protect her? Brandon? Or those rapists on their way to Vegas? Lake is out there trying to look cute while playing in the slop.*

Samara thinks of Abuela Lola and the community she built not only in getting each other jobs, but warning each other of the monsters they needed to stay away from—even when the beasts might be living right in the same house. There's power in the collective voice, in telling the truth. Samara is about to lay out everything she's seen that night for everyone to hear because honestly, who fucking cares about Antonio Mota, his clothes, Lake, or anyone else? There are only the women in front of her right now and how they tend to each other, how they care even for her, a stranger in their city.

The Ramona dress she's wearing is ripped in multiple places and soiled. There is a large tear on the hem and the choker is holding on only by the tiniest scrap of leather. Mascara streams down her cheeks. Scratches line her arms. Every muscle in her body is clenched tight. Although her mind tells her she's safe, her body is still ready to run, expecting Brandon to appear again with his charming lies.

Suddenly, all the sewing machines turn on without the aid of anyone. No one else seems to even notice this, each person too busy tending to Rosa or waiting for help to arrive.

Dolores pulls away from the group. Samara follows as the seamstress walks over to her workstation. The seamstress drapes fabric onto a dressmaker form. Her actions are performed without fuss, an exercise in the familiar. It seems to bring her a tiny bit of calm. Her work is a salve, her balm for when there is disorder.

Samara slumps down on a chair and watches her. For the first time since she began working here, she can accept that it wasn't coldness Dolores displayed but a coat of protection, a mask to cover the fear. Work for the seamstress is a repose, something she can control. Her fingers on the fabric save her.

Samara catches the name sewn alongside the seam of the dress Dolores fiddles with. It doesn't matter whether the seamstress can see the name. It never did.

She listens to the familiar hum the machines make; how Samara's missed it. How she used to love hiding underneath her grandmother's sewing machine. A whole world she created below her while life was happening above her.

In the far distance, the wail of sirens can be heard, but Samara is only attuned to the sewing machines. She closes her eyes and allows the sound to finally comfort her.

ACKNOWLEDGMENTS

Tiny Threads was my way of grappling with the disturbing realities we're all currently living in. During dark times, scary tales provide me with a sense of comfort and control. Although the Vernon I write about in this book is purely fictional, factories have been poisoning brown communities for decades, while powerful men believe that their sexual predations are a right. Truth can always be found in the horrific.

Special thanks goes to the MacDowell Colony, where this novel was completed while staring out at a sometimes-wintery forest. I have such deep gratitude for my editor, Tricia Narwani, and the rest of the Del Rey team for launching my adult debut novel with tenderness and patience. The stunning cover design by Rachel Ake is both sinister and sexy. As always, thanks to my literary agent, Eddie Schneider, who has helped me navigate my publishing career since day one.

I love you, David, Sophia, Isabelle, Annabel, Angie, Brandy,

Marisa, Elisa, Jean, Jade, Kima, Evan, Marytza, Jaquira, Carolina, Aditi, and anyone who listened to me work through this haunting story.

Finally, I would like to thank the nightmares that led me to talk in my sleep. I still finished this novel in spite of them.

ABOUT THE AUTHOR

LILLIAM RIVERA is a MacDowell Fellow and an award-winning author of eight works of fiction: four young adult novels, three middle grade books, and a graphic novel for DC Comics. Her books have been awarded a Pura Belpré honor and featured on NPR and in *The New Yorker,* the *Los Angeles Times, The New York Times,* and multiple "best of" lists. Her novel *Never Look Back* is slated for an Amazon movie adaptation. A Bronx, New York, native, Lilliam Rivera currently lives in Los Angeles.

lilliamrivera.com

Instagram: @lilliamr

ABOUT THE TYPE

This book was set in Dante, a typeface designed by Giovanni Mardersteig (1892–1977). Conceived as a private type for the Officina Bodoni in Verona, Italy, Dante was originally cut only for hand composition by Charles Malin, the famous Parisian punch cutter, between 1946 and 1952. Its first use was in an edition of Boccaccio's *Trattatello in laude di Dante* that appeared in 1954. The Monotype Corporation's version of Dante followed in 1957. Though modeled on the Aldine type used for Pietro Cardinal Bembo's treatise *De Aetna* in 1495, Dante is a thoroughly modern interpretation of that venerable face.